SHE had come
from the country
to become
a lady . . .
Suddenly, she
was working as
a spy!

Stephanie

a novel by

CAROLINE ARNETT

FAWCETT CREST • NEW YORK

STEPHANIE

Published by Fawcett Crest Books, a unit of CBS Publications, the Consumer Publishing Division of CBS Inc.

Copyright © 1979 by Caroline Arnett

ISBN: 0-449-24081-9

Selection of the Doubleday Romance Library

Printed in the United States of America

10   9   8   7   6   5   4   3   2   1

Chapter 1

THE door of the slowly moving coach opened and a dark figure slid out of the night and on to the seat beside her. The small lamps at the box seat revealed only a white blur of a face.

"What . . . what . . . are you . . . doing . . . here, sir?" The words came out in a breathless flutter.

"Joining you in your coach," said a pleasant voice, "and grateful it is moving with the speed of a turtle."

"If . . . if . . . it is my jewels . . . you seek . . . I have none." The voice quivered uncertainly.

"No. No jewels are desired, ma'am." He sounded amused. "I merely seek a means of transportation into town and yours is the only coach on the road."

"That is because I left early. But a gentleman should be able to manage on his own." Indignation banished the flutter.

"Quite true. But I departed in a hurry and could not locate the friend who brought me."

"But why did you have to leave quickly?" Curiosity had banished the indignation.

"Because I was found in a place where I should not be. No, not in a lady's bed as you are doubtless assuming. I was trapped in Lord Bampton's study and had to leave by the window."

"How enterprising and what fun," she gasped.

"Yes, since I was successful. I am gratified you approve. But I had a devil of a time retrieving my cloak and vanishing down the driveway. Fortunately those masses of untrimmed rhododendrons gave me shadow, and the gates were untended. I was almost resigned to shank's mare when I heard this vehicle advancing at a stately pace and waited and was overjoyed to find only one occupant." He was talking easily, giving her time to recover from her surprise, though that was less than he had expected. "I am fortunate she is so charming."

"Don't try to cozzen me. You have no notion if I am charming," she said a little tartly.

"But your voice is. That is enough for our ride together."

"You are assuming that I will permit you to remain."

"Of course, because you are kind and would not condemn me to walking all these miles."

"I could scream," she offered thoughtfully.

"To whom? There is no one to hear you but the coachman and he is probably deaf or has learned to be to such sounds. You are quite safe, I assure you."

"I am sure you are right about him," she agreed with a touch of bitterness. "Nothing that belongs to that bottlehead Freddie Minnly could behave properly, including himself."

"So this is his coach. Yes, I last saw him quite drunk on a sofa."

"Exactly. And he could not sober up and I didn't want him to for just before he collapsed he kept saying he was taking me to his own house. So I saw nothing for it but to take his coach and leave him."

"Very sensible. I wonder you succeeded."

"Oh, I found a side door and went to the coach yard and found the shabbiest one there and told the man he was to take me as I directed and then return for his master. I had to speak to him very firmly, but it worked. And that's the best escort my aunt could find for me." Her bitterness was very apparent now.

"Pity. I can tell you deserve better. But why Minnly?" There was idle interest under his amusement.

"Because he sometimes frequents Mrs Riffton's where she goes to gamble. And it is my belief," she added darkly, "that he lost money to my aunt and that is how she made him escort me to this affair tonight. My first ball, too! In London, that is."

"Did you enjoy it?"

"Of course not, with that ramshackle fop. I had hoped to meet other people. But either he didn't know any one or no one wished to know him. We danced twice and he did bring me a little supper but mostly he sat on the sofa by me and drank and yammered about his life in London. I was ashamed to be seen with him."

"Unpleasant for you. But it was hardly the thing for you to go to a ball at a strange house without a chaperon."

"I knew it was wrong. But Aunt Edita said I was being country-missish and that things were done differently in London and if she approved I could not question her judgement. I'm sure she only did it to silence my questions about the routs and soirées she had promised."

"But how did it all come about? Come, we have at least an hour ride before us. We are strangers. We can't see each other, would never recognize each other. You obviously need someone to talk to. Why not tell me how you come to be in this fix?"

She sighed. "It is true I have no one to talk to for Hester is a dear girl but cowed. But no, I know nothing of you except you are a gentleman by your voice and must be a thief."

"We'll forget that. Let us tell our first names so we do not speak just to space. My name is Roone. Tell me yours and then of your plight. Speaking aloud is often comforting."

"Mine is Stephanie," she said hesitantly. "It might help to talk. I know no one in town and would dearly love to return to Dorset but I won't because that would please Aunt Edita and infuriate and distress my grandfather."

"Two good reasons not to go. But how came you here anyway, poor child?"

The warmth and sympathy in his voice quite undid her. It would be a comfort to talk to someone who was no one. She wished she could see the face that went with the easy voice. She sighed. The coach gave a lurch and a gentle hand steadied her. "It is a wearying tale, I fear, for a stranger."

"It will help pass a wearying journey for us both. What has become of your flutter?"

"I only talk like that now when I am surprised. It was to please grandfather at first."

"Why was that?"

"Because grandmother had fluttered and pretended she was so timid only he could protect her. He had been a famous soldier. He loved her dearly, you see, and only partly realized that in all her flutterings she was guiding him in every aspect. When I was small I imitated her and grandfather was amused and I found it often worked well to get my own way. Since grandmother died it is mother who guides him."

"How does she manage?"

"She is fragile and vague, and truly not at all strong, but always knows what is best. They are both such darlings."

"I am sure. Your flutterings got you to London?"

"Only in part. They both wanted me to come, they felt it right after a year at school in Bath. But they have no connections in London any more. When Aunt Edita wrote in her yearly letter last November that she was introducing her daughter to society this next season grandfather offered her a good sum if she would introduce me also."

"Quite logical. But it didn't work?"

There came another sigh. "No. And I can't bear to tell the poor dears that it is all a miserable fraud. She always wrote of affairs she attended and mentioned names and they, away from London for so many years, believed her."

"They didn't know her?"

"Not at all. She claims to be a distant cousin of my father's—I am instructed to call her Aunt—and that she was at the wedding, which was quite large, but no one remembers her. Then, when my father was killed, he was a captain, mother and I returned to Laneleet to live. Aunt Edita sent a note of sympathy and announced she had married a Mr Tinkham but did not admit he was a business man in the city. Mother acknowledged the note and thereafter Aunt Edita wrote about once a year, to keep track of the family she said but she must have had some future gain in mind."

"Which came in the form of money from your grandfather. I do not recognize the name Tinkham."

"No gentleman would. Her claim to move in high society was completely false. In fact," and the words burst out, "she is a liar and a thief, for I know grandfather sent a good sum and I was only allowed four gowns and they were made at the house and are not at all the thing. I know from mother and school what is fourth rate."

"Assuredly. The season has just commenced. What has she done for you?"

"We went to a public concert of music by Mr Handel. And to a rout at a Mrs Alworth that was crowded with loud overdressed people and Hester and I were introduced only to some men who looked and acted like clerks. There is no abigail for us and the housekeeper, a most unappetizing and unpleasant creature, has gone with us three times to Bond Street to look at the shops and we were given only five shillings to spend."

"Hardly sufficient. Yours is a sad tale, my girl, and I can see you are in a bind. No young men have come to the house?"

"Freddie came once to ask me to this affair and acted like a cornered rat all the time. But," and Stephanie's voice took on a sudden vivacity, "Aunt Edita did invite Sir Andrew Seddon to tea on a Sunday afternoon a week ago. He is the most beautiful young man, with perfect manners, and entirely new to London. She found him at Mrs Riffton's and learned he knew no one in town and he was grateful for any kindness. He comes from Suffolk."

"Did he tell you how he came to be here?" Roone asked idly.

"Yes. He is open about everything. He was sent from Portugal, because of a wound, to the staff of some lord at the Admiralty. Aunt Edita is taking me to Mrs Riffton's on Friday night for he will be there. But, oh, it is all so dull and different from what was promised and what I'd hoped for—balls and opera and new people and adventures of one kind or another. My brother and I had splendid adventures together when we were young. I would do anything for one now."

"I suggest you exercise discretion about that anything."

She paid that no heed. "You must be thinking I am spineless not to try to correct my situation, but I truly do not know what to do. I do not wish my grandfather to learn his plans have so completely miscarried for he and my mother would be so distressed and might come to London and they are not adequately strong for the journey and the encounters that would result here. You can see I am at a standstill."

"I do indeed, and I regret I cannot come up with any solution. Perhaps things will better themselves. If not, you had better contrive to return to Dorset for you will continue to be miserable here. What is your direction? We have passed Hyde Park."

"On Eldon Street, number 29, not far from Bedford Street."

"You have told the coachman? Good. The next time we halt I will leave you. I must thank you, Stephanie, for the ride and your most absorbing tale. When this linkboy passes I will be gone. I wish you good luck and a way out of your difficulties."

The coach slowed because of one ahead, the door opened, a dark figure slid into the night, the door closed. As the coach moved again Stephanie thought of some of the things she should have asked the man instead of pouring out her woes, and dismissed him in favor of contemplating how she would report the evening to Aunt Edita, omitting, of course, the ride home.

Chapter 2

HAVING mentioned Sir Andrew Seddon, inevitably he was in Stephanie's mind even while she told Aunt Edita roundly that the highly-touted ball had been a disaster, which she described in detail, and why she had come home alone.

"You're an ungrateful girl." Aunt Edita came near to screeching. "I arrange this treat for you and you complain. You are too highty-tighty. Go to your room."

"Happily," Stephanie told her with dignity, "but never allow that Freddie to come near me again."

To Hester Sephanie poured out her account of the evening and in the process recovered much of her customary good humor and began to laugh. "Now I can see it was funny, but it was not at the time. I know I am a veritable innocent when it comes to London, but I know enough to realize that Freddie is not at all the thing. Nor, for that matter, is Mrs Riffton's."

"Mother has never taken me there," Hester said sadly. "It would be a change. She says I do not know how to comport myself."

"I'm not sure I do, but I go to meet Sir Andrew. I am sure he is the only gentleman in the place."

Hester's blue eyes glowed. "He is so handsome and so kind. I could hardly refrain from watching him all the time."

"Asking him to tea is the only thing your mother has done for us." Stephanie's gray eyes held a spark of anger as she gave a violent brush to her hair. "He said he was green to London, you remember. There is no knowing what will happen to him."

"But he is a baronet," Hester protested.

"That signifies nothing, and he only inherited a few months ago. He said he was raised in Suffolk quite simply. If it had not been a family tradition that the oldest son go into the army he might never have left the place. He is more an innocent than I am."

"Surely he will learn. His manners are impeccable and his observations intelligent."

"He would, given the right opportunity." Stephanie frowned. "Since he has no friends in town, as he told us, and no one to advise him, it is we who must stand his friends."

"Oh." Hester gave a squeak of surprise. "We have no friends either."

"And we are handicapped, if you will forgive me,

by living with your mother. How we may guide Sir Andrew I do not know, but he is much too beautiful and too nice to be allowed to fall into the wrong company. He will trust us, I am convinced."

A faint pink at the thought came into Hester's pale cheeks. "I do not see how that will come about."

"It will. Something will happen," Stephanie assured her confidently. "And, anyway, I will see him on Friday."

But the meeting at Mrs Riffton's, Stephanie felt, was not at all satisfactory. Sir Andrew came up to her where she sat a little to one side of Aunt Edita at the whist table and his face showed such pleasure her heart turned over. It was allowed they might stroll around the gaming rooms but there was little chance for converse as they both became occupied watching the play and the people at the various tables and admitting in whispers their lack of comprehension. In less than half an hour they were summoned to Aunt Edita who announced the cards were against her and she was leaving. Sir Andrew's disappointment was evident for a flash, which again was warming, but he bowed and said he was delighted to accept the invitation to tea the following Sunday.

He seemed a little abstracted during that ritual, though he listened to Aunt Edita's strictures on modern manners and the perils of whist with polite attention. As soon as the two cups were drunk he begged permission to escort the two girls for a walk to Russell Square. Since that was a spot of eminent respectability, surrounded as it was by the solid mansions of wealthy merchants, permission was graciously granted and the girls happily donned cloaks and bonnets which Stephanie thought extremely homely. But Sir Andrew's responses to their comments on shops and people were desultory and once at the square Stephanie turned to him impulsively.

"You are distressed by something, sir. Do you not wish to tell us? Frequently a worry shared with friends is explained away."

The gratitude in the deep blue eyes was rewarding. "I am grateful for your perception, Miss Langley, for I would like the advice of you and Miss Tinkham but I was not sure it was a matter I should mention to you."

"You may mention anything, sir," Hester said in her soft voice, "for between friends there need be no hesitation."

"That is my feeling," he agreed, "And since you have been so kind as to become my friends I do wish to turn to you."

"Just begin," urged Stephanie as he paused. "Where was it?"

"At Mrs Riffton's," he began slowly. "It is about a girl."

"Of course," she said as she heard Hester's soft gasp. "What did she do?"

"It was after you left, Miss Langley. I was watching the roulette table when someone brushed by me. I turned and saw a girl in red standing alone, a handkerchief falling from her hand. Of course I retrieved it and offered it to her. As she thanked me I could see tears in her eyes. I bowed and asked if she would like to retire to one of those sofas in the alcoves, for her distress was about to become obvious, and offered her my arm."

"That was gallant of you," murmured Hester.

"But only proper. Our mother always told us that a gentleman should come to the aid of any lady at any time. Our mother has seen to it that I and my brothers have proper manners."

She has done well, thought Stephanie, but some things could be carried too far. "What then?" she prompted.

"As we seated ourselves I asked if I might procure her a glass of lemonade. She put a hand on my arm and begged me not to leave her for if I did a man she feared would take my place. So I asked who she feared and she nodded toward an old, wrinkled man with a big nose who was watching us. I was at a loss to know what to do," he said simply, "so I did nothing. In a moment she began to say in a low voice that he had offered for her and her mother was constantly urging her to accept him because of his wealth, and she could not, even to save the fortunes of her family.

"To distract her mind I said she must have many suitors.

" 'But none so wealthy,' she said with despair.

"I said she should hold firm. Then, to my surprise, she begged me to come to her home on Tuesday evening and persuade her mother that she—she said her name was Juliana—should choose her own husband. I was taken aback, I must say. She clasped her hands and gave a sob and said she had no one to stand up for her and her mother would listen to a gentleman. I was fearful she would draw attention and did not know how to say no as she gave me her direction. A dumpy woman with an unpleasant face came up, scolded Juliana for making an exhibition of herself and told me they would expect me on Tuesday at nine. Since I had risen, I just bowed and walked away."

"You had not agreed to call," Stephanie pointed out brightly.

"True. If that woman had not arrived I might have agreed, for I was sorry for the girl, and as I walked away I wondered if it was my duty to help Juliana. After a few minutes I decided I had remained a sufficient time and went for my hat and stick."

"Something else happened," Stephanie said gleefully.

"Yes. The woman knowing about the Tuesday invitation had put me off. And then, glancing in a mirror, I saw Juliana and the woman and the man laughing together. What do you ladies advise?"

"Is Juliana pretty?" Hester asked sadly.

"Some might think so," he allowed, "but for me she had too much color on her face and her gown was cut in a fashion I would not care to see on my sister. But if she is truly being forced into a distasteful marriage perhaps one should aid her."

The tale had carried them halfway around the square. Stephanie glanced at the houses, each with its front steps newly washed, its windows shielded by heavy draperies and each with an air of self-congratulation. These merchants would never have been caught by such a plea. Obviously innocent young men should not be turned loose in London, but Sir Andrew was not stupid.

"There is nothing you can do to help her," she said firmly, "even if what she said is true. The woman would not be influenced by the Regent himself, unless he paid her in gold."

Sir Andrew halted, laughing a little, his eyes crinkling at the corners. "That is what I hoped to hear from you. I know one cannot go through life being suspicious, but I was, from the outset."

"Oh, why?" lilted Hester.

"The handkerchief. At a dance at Woodbridge last year a girl did the same thing, but she was a friend and just wanted me to dance with her. She confessed it was one of the oldest of tricks, but it often worked, for there I was dancing with her."

"You were so right to be suspicious this time," Stephanie told him gaily. "You must not go near the house. It is a trap."

He laughed again. "If it is it would catch only a minnow for I have neither wealth nor position. It would be amusing to see their faces when I told them that."

"But not worth the danger of some kind of entanglement. You truly would not have gone?"

"Not in the end. But I thought I might tell you ladies, and amuse you, and ask your advice."

Stephanie pushed back the horrid bonnet. "Of course you must not go. And if you see Juliana again merely bow and do not fall into converse with her for she might bring out some other Banbury tale that might be awkward."

"You are right. I am grateful to you both. How fortunate I am to have such good friends." He stopped and took off his hat and bowed, a gleam of sunlight landing on his dark blond hair.

Delighted, the girls gave a little dip. "And we are fortunate to have you for a friend," breathed Hester, starry-eyed.

"Indeed," Stephanie agreed, "for you are our only means of going for a walk of a Sunday." Appalled at all her thoughtless words implied she flung out a hand in protest, but Sir Andrew was laughing again and pointing out it was delightful to be of some use to two charming young ladies. So Stephanie said they were in his debt and by then they were back at the Tinkham house.

The two girls congratulated themselves, rather complacently, on the rescue of Sir Andrew. They were rather disappointed when he reported the next Sunday that Juliana had been escorted by a middle-aged merchant and, with a top-lofty air, had cut him dead.

Chapter 3

ESHAM Roone Calthorpe, fifth Baron Airde, returned to his house on Cavendish Square one evening much earlier than was his custom. He had been bored at Lady Sherland's. The music had been of poor quality, the people dull, the food to come would be pretentious and tasteless, he knew, and why, he had asked himself suddenly, should he subject himself to so many inconveniences at once. There was no need. He had allowed himself of recent months to attend too many such affairs which held nothing of interest, and vowed he would cut line in the future. Pleading another engagement, he had wandered home through the quiet West End streets now occasionally lighted by the new lamps put up by the city. There was no need to disturb the servants so he turned in the small side door on the alley which led to the stables. A lighted candle waited in the narrow hall, for he had the door left unlocked when he was out for the evening. He mounted the narrow stairs set in the wall and strolled along the carpeted hall towards his own suite and paused. More light than usual filled the doorway and he heard a faint rustle, then stood in the doorway watching.

A brown-haired girl in a blue dress was sitting at his desk turning over a pile of papers she had evidently taken from the open bottom drawer. A fist landed on the pile and she said "Bother" quite loudly, picking up the heap and thrusting it back in the drawer, half turning to open the one on the other side.

"Perhaps if you will tell me what you're looking for I'll be able to help you," he suggested agreeably.

She whirled around in the chair, both hands going to her cheeks in a gesture of fright and grey eyes widened. "S . . . s . . . sir, you startled me," the voice stuttered and halted, the hands dropped.

"Evidently. But two can cover more papers than one." He moved a little into the room. The candelabra on the desk, the drum table, the mantelpiece lighted her curls and the curves of her cheeks. "Perhaps it is also something I seek."

"Why . . . why do you say that? You . . . you must wonder at my being here." The voice fluttered a little breathlessly.

"Not at all. Papers are so often mislaid. You came in by the side door, I take it."

"Oh . . oh yes. Lord Maleby told Sir Andrew it was

always left open of an evening and how to reach this room. So . . . it is very important for our country." She looked at him bravely.

"I am sure," he soothed. "Who told you?"

"Sir Andrew. And he's in the government. But he felt he couldn't come himself . . . that would look so odd."

"So he enlisted your aid. What papers are they?" His calm and his smile seemed to reassure her.

"I . . . I don't know. But any that have a little red circle in the upper left corner . . . I promised not to read them."

"Of course. I'd be glad to find them also." He sat down on the arm of a wing chair. "Stop fluttering, Stephanie, and tell me why you came like a thief in the night."

She frowned, then her face, a piquant one with a short nose between high cheek bones above a mouth delectably curved, cleared and she laughed. "You're Roone, the man who cadged a ride two weeks ago. You had me quite nervous for a moment."

"So you showed, most attractively. That was what gave you away. We do seem to meet in unusual circumstances, don't we?"

"I've never been in a man's house alone before," she told him with dignity. "You are doubtless out to steal something."

"I don't doubt you, but what brought you here?" The quiet voice was somehow reassuring.

"My patriotic duty, and my desire to take care of Sir Andrew," she said happily. "He asked my help— and of course it was something different to do."

"So I see. But what is it about?"

"He told me only a little. He said he has been told someone is stealing government papers, orders, plans about troop movements to—to Portugal or beyond the seas, and when supply ships will be leaving our ports. Then the papers, or information, gets to the French so they can send out their ships at the right time."

"But why come here?"

"Sir Andrew said he was told it was the owner of this house who might be guilty, have the missing papers. The direction was given him and how to enter of an evening for the owner is always out. He was to look through the desk, and any box, so I came for him."

"How did you get away from your Aunt Edita?"

"To deceive me about going into Society she asked him to escort me to a crush at a Mrs Shafley's. It was an odd mixture of people and I am sure not real society at all." She paused and frowned. "We were hardly there when he took me to a window seat and explained his orders to me and that he needed my help because he was sure that if he were found going through papers in a gentleman's house he would be cashiered, and he was sure I, as a daughter and granddaughter and sister of soldiers, would wish to help my country. It was an adventure dropped in my lap. So we came here by hackney and he is waiting outside and we will return to the party. But what are you doing here, Roone?"

"You might say I am after the same papers." One long finger was tapping his knee as he thoughtfully watched the vivid face.

"Are you sure it isn't the plate or jewelry you are after?" Suspicion was strong in her voice.

"Quite sure. Plate is so awkward to steal and it never brings what it is worth. Same with jewelry, even the best. Well, pull out the other drawer and I'll go through this one. You must be able to tell Sir Andrew you have been thorough."

"But which of us will get them if we find them?" she demanded as her hand hovered.

"We'll decide that if we do." He pulled a straight-back chair beside the desk as she tugged at the bottom drawer.

"These look like letters," she exclaimed doubtfully.

"Just sift through them. Your honor wouldn't let you read them and anyway you haven't time." Now he was close he could see a few faint freckles across her nose and that the brown curls were held by a half buried ribbon of matching blue, and her arms white as she plunged both into the deep drawer.

In a moment she raised her head. "These are all letters. Do you think they are love letters? I've never had a love letter," she added wistfully. "I suppose ladies do write them, but I've never known a man as would be worth the trouble of reading what he has written."

"They're family and business," he said absently, "kept for future self-protection and probably not worth the quill that wrote them."

"There are no papers here." She straightened and shoved back the drawer. "And these small drawers have letter paper."

"You'll find bills in the black box on the table," he directed amusedly. "Don't read them. There. Your duty is done." He rose. "You are sure Sir Andrew is waiting?"

"He is around the corner. He would never leave me."

"Perhaps he will have other—adventures for you," Roone offered slowly.

"Oh, I hope so. It is exciting to get into a big house. I only wish I had time to look in the rooms . . ." There was a question in her voice.

"Most unwise. You might encounter a servant. Is that your cloak? Bring it and I'll see you to the door. I came the same way, you see."

"You aren't going to look anywhere else?" She paused as the thin blue silk fell around her. "I'll have to stay if you are."

"No. Word of honor I'll do no more searching." He picked up a single candlestick and guided her to the hall, the side stairs, the door. "You're sure you're all right?" he asked doubtfully.

"Of course. And thank you for your help. It has been a pleasure to encounter you again."

He gave a sudden chuckle. "What a well brought up girl you are, Stephanie. I look forward to our next meeting." He opened the door for her, closed it, opened it again and stepped out into a shadow and waited. The light footsteps sped down the alley, halted, and there was the rumble of a hackney getting under way. He returned upstairs and stood looking at his desk, one finger tapping the surface. Now what was that all about? It was gratifying to discover that Stephanie was as charming and appealing as she had sounded in that coach.

Something smokey was going on about some government papers, apparently at the Admiralty. When given his post he had been told to keep an eye out for anything out of the ordinary because he had, when in Portugal, uncovered some very shady doings. This was all odd enough to beg for his attention. But why should Maleby choose this house? Was it just to flush a cover and see if any pheasant rose? It seemed unlikely his lordship would wish his own aide to fall into hot soup. Roone frowned. It was true Maleby disliked him intensely. There had been the business of his being given the post at the Foreign Office in part because of his acclaimed military career—when the Prince Regent had been trying to obtain it for his dear friend Maleby. Then he had cut out Maleby with that dashing Bird of Paradise, for a brief spell, and his horse had won a race a year ago, and though it was unlikely Maleby had learned he had been blackballed at a club as an upstart not fit for the company of certain gentlemen he might have gleaned a hint. But this search for nonexistent papers here showed a vindictiveness out of the ordinary.

It was something to be pursued and the only trail led to Aunt Edita and Sir Andrew. He had the name Tinkham, the cit Aunt Edita had married, and Mrs Riffton where she went to gamble and Sir Andrew was found. Roone nodded at the desk and went to the library for his customary glass of port and some pages of Clarendon's History.

For Mrs Riffton's Roone dressed somberly in black coat, gray pantaloons and unobtrusive neckcloth and took his sword cane, since the address was beyond Tottenham Court Road. He went by hackney. The man at the double doors bowed slightly, after a quick glance, and motioned to the cloakroom on the right and the stairs beyond. A once-pretty woman smiled coquettishly as she took his things. "New, aren't you, sir?" she asked.

"Kindly put my things near at hand," he directed, "in case I wish to leave early."

"You won't wish that, sir, not if you seek high play," and added an "Oooh" as he slipped a crown into her hand.

The stairs ended in a short hall that led to the main saloon, a red-damask and mirror-walled room with chandeliers suspended above four tables. "Your name, sir?" an unctous voice housed in a portly black clad butler oozed beside him. "So I may inform Mrs Riffton of your arrival."

"Mr Roone," he told the man. "I will stroll a few minutes before I decide where to play."

"You'll find roulette, sir, vingt-et-un, loo, macao, what you wish, and whist in side rooms. There are smaller rooms for greater privacy and higher stakes upstairs."

Roone nodded and strolled through the draped doorway. Within ten steps he was confronted by a hawk-faced woman in cloth of gold topped by an impossibly blond wig. "Mr Roone," she gushed. "So kind of you to favor us. May I introduce you to any of the tables —persons?"

He bowed very slightly. "Most kind of you to offer, ma'am. But I would prefer to look around before I settle on my game tonight." He bowed again and moved away toward the cashier where he purchased a hundred pounds worth of counters and then began to wander around the edge of the room. Now he could see that the gold-braid trim and the sconces were tarnished, the satin of draperies worn, and mirrors and crystals dusty. The roulette table was popular, onlookers crowding around the players, all middle-class. The whole effect of the place was ambitiously tawdry and ill-kept. The impassive croupiers were thoroughly professional and the dealer at vingt-et-un had fingers of an almost impossible nimbleness. Then, through an arch, he glimpsed a table of whist and, facing the large room, a middle-aged female in dark red satin and intricate black wig and a little behind her a girl in pale blue watching everything brightly. He moved nearer. It was Stephanie so the imposing figure must be Aunt Edita. He stepped to one side of the arch and Stephanie saw him, quickly rose and spoke to her aunt and passed him without a sign. Around the corner he caught up with her.

"Well done," he approved. "Can we talk anywhere?"

She held out her hand. "Roone! What a surprise! I offered to bring my aunt a glass of punch, which can take a time to procure."

"I did not expect to see you here," he commented, as they turned away.

"Sir Andrew said at tea he hoped to see me this evening, so Aunt Edita brought me. This time several men have asked to be introduced," she added with a twinkle, "and for me to stand by them while they play, but she put them off. They were not attractive," she added thoughtfully.

"I am not surprised. They are a rather scruffy lot, here."

"That is how they appeared to me," she said swiftly, "even though I know so little of London. But then, to see Sir Andrew is worth anything. But what brings you here?"

He laughed a little. "Curiosity. Have you been on any more adventures with your Sir Andrew?"

"He is not mine, though I wish he were. He is attached to Lord Maleby at the Admiralty. But I always hope, perhaps tonight . . ." She halted a moment and looked around the room. "Anything would be better than this, or just sitting home reading, or listening to Hester's longings to live in the country, which she has never done or she wouldn't moon on about it."

Roone looked down at her with some compassion. Her eyes shone with eagerness and her tumbled curls were charming though not modishly cut, but her gown was sleazy silk and not well made with ill-sewn ruffles at neck and sleeves and hem that tried to make it appear the latest cry. Suddenly her eyes widened and she clutched Roone's arm with both hands.

"There he is," she breathed. "Isn't he beautiful?"

Roone looked up. Standing in the doorway was one of the most beautiful young men he had ever seen. The eyes were large beneath arched brows, the nose straight, mouth well cut, the chin firm, the blond hair waved a little, his bones were obviously good and there was no hint of pride or self-consciousness on a face whose whole was even better than its parts. Stephanie was gazing entranced, lips a little apart, face glowing.

"Stephanie," Roone said sharply. "Stop looking at him that way. Do you want the world to read your heart? Look at me. He will find you. Yes, he is beautiful. I had not believed you. Now, smile and say something. And tell me your name, I will need it to address you."

She promptly gazed at him and smiled widely. "I knew you would agree if you saw him. My name is Langley. Oh, he is coming toward us."

"Don't notice him yet. You must learn to behave properly. Introduce us when he arrives."

"Miss Langley. What luck!" The eager voice was matched by a neat bow. "I hardly dared hope to find you here."

"Sir Andrew. How pleasant to see you." She was quite composed now. "May I make you known to each other? Mr Roone, Sir Andrew Seddon."

"Delighted to meet you, sir." Roone bowed a little. Close at hand the face was as fine as at a distance, the eyes were blue and candid. How had this nice young man come to this place he wondered, as Sir Andrew bowed again, took out his snuffbox, offered it, nodded as Sir Andrew declined and put it away. "Miss Langley tells me you are new to London," he said affably.

Sir Andrew laughed. "Indeed, I am the veriest greenhorn. And only here by chance, and Captain Thringwood's bad luck."

"Which was lucky for you. What happened?"

"Lord Maleby requested he be detached from active service and added to his own staff. He was waiting for passage when he went out fox hunting and his horse refused a fence, fell on him, and broke both his legs. I was just getting over a shoulder wound, not back in the lines, you see, so my general told me to come in his place."

"Was . . . was your wound serious, sir?" Stephanie's question fluttered a little.

"Nothing to speak of. Just laid me up a bit. I told the general I knew nothing of London but he said that didn't matter, Maleby would tell me what to do, so a passage was found in three days."

"Does he keep you busy?" Roone asked idly.

"Oh, yes. I write orders, dispatches as he directs, carry them around, and, and do other things." The blue eyes turned to smile at Stephanie.

Roone groaned inwardly. The man was an innocent and too openly honest to be mixed up in anything dubious. He reached out an arm and took a glass of punch from the tray of a passing waiter. "Here, Miss Langley, take this to your aunt as you offered and tell her you are walking around with Sir Andrew."

"Why . . . why . . yes," she fluttered again. "How clever of you." Carrying the glass very carefully she went toward the side room. Both men watched the slender figure.

"How did you learn of Mrs Riffton's, since you are new to London?" He hoped the question sounded like idle curtesy.

"Captain Thringwood told me I would be doing odd errands, such as coming here, and not to make a cake of myself and object or ask questions, which I would not have anyway. I went to call on him before I sailed. He wasn't a whit pleased to see me." The fine brows puckered a little. "Almost made me feel I'd been responsible for his horse falling. Told me to explain all to Lord Maleby and say he'd be over as soon as he could walk."

"But you wisely took time to get proper garb," approved Roone. The clothes were conservative and not very expensive.

"I'd been going to ask Captain Thringwood about that, but I didn't like to for he was not at all forthcoming to me. So I went to another Captain, Willingdon, a splendid chap, and he gave me the names of a tailor and a bootmaker, said they weren't the tops but would do well by me. I hate to think what the tops would have cost me. Do I look all right, sir? I haven't met a gentleman I could consult."

"You do," Roone assured him. "Very much all right. You come from . . . ?" He thought about that last sentence.

"Suffolk, not far from Sudbury. Do you know that part of the country, sir?" he asked eagerly, and sobered as Roone shook his head. "It is lovely," he added wistfully.

"Aunt just nodded when I told her," Stephanie told them happily. "So now I can go anywhere. She must be winning for she was quite agreeable." Her bright eyes were on Sir Andrew. Roone touched her foot lightly. She glanced at him, wide-eyed, caught his slight shake, and looked down.

"Should we play?" Sir Andrew's tone was a little anxious. "I know nothing about it, but . . ."

"We'll walk around and watch." Roone steered them toward the roulette table where he mentioned a few of the rules, guided them past the loo and chemin-de-fer, with a warning not to try such, halted at the vingt-et-un, which intimidated them by the speed of the play, and so back to roulette.

"Here," he took two seats just vacated, "You can try your luck," and pulled out the counters and divided them, and placed himself behind their chairs.

"These aren't money." Stephanie half turned and looked up with a faint frown. "I thought people gambled for money."

"These are just counters," he whispered back. "Pick any number or color you choose."

"Then it doesn't matter if I lose," she said gaily and leaned forward to put a counter on red.

He let them play until all the counters were gone, which was quite promptly, and took them away. "That is enough for the first time."

"Oh, yes, even though counters aren't money I hated to see them swept up that way." Stephanie brushed her fingers together. "I don't think I could be happy gambling."

Sir Andrew was thoughtful. "It seems to me a foolish way to lose money."

"You are both right, so hold to those notions," Roone told them seriously but his eyes were amused.

"Thank you for giving us a chance to try the game." Sir Andrew was appealingly grateful. "I never would have on my own."

"My advice is to stay away from such establishments as this, for if one goes one must play a little." He moved them to a sofa in an alcove and after expressing his pleasure at the encounter, departed. The major-domo bowed him out with the air due one who has lost but not largely and the porter summoned a hackney.

Something would have to be done about Stephanie and her Sir Andrew, Roone decided in the jolting musty interior. She was too gay and delightful a girl to be left in such a havey-cavey situation, the man too innocent to rescue her himself, and his instructions from Lord Maleby too peculiar to be ignored. Though it was true there were spies and sympathizers with the French and information did leak across the channel, it was doubtful if there were ever any official papers marked with a red circle—unless Maleby himself put it on some. He must be on some ploy of his own. As for Stephanie, it was clear he should make a visit to Dorset. Roone was so deep in thought the hackney took him by his house and around the square before he roused and called a halt.

As Roone left them Stephanie searched wildly for an acceptable topic of conversation, but Sir Andrew smoothly began to comment on London, for he walked the streets when his time was his own, and since she was not so permitted she listened with absorption, sure her views would match his. When she saw Mrs Tinkham approaching she interrupted and asked him to tea again on Sunday and so informed her hostess, who kindly approved.

As the cobblestones rattled beneath the wheels of the old coach, and Aunt Edita's voice rattled above them, Stephanie was absorbed in the two faces filling her mind's eye. "Beautiful" was not a word to be used for a man, she knew, but there was no other for Sir Andrew, and he was so engagingly nice that the combination was almost unbelievable. Beside him Roone could not be considered handsome. His dark brows were straight, his dark hair had only the slightest wave, his mouth was too wide and as firm as his chin, the hazel eyes were striking but too cool, not at all expressive like Sir Andrew's, and the hollows of the cheeks were too pronounced. Yet he had an air of complete ease and one could but sense underneath a strength which was bewildering for it did not match his quiet surface. She surveyed her vocabulary and decided distinguished might fit him, though that made him an enigma because of his self-confessed occupation as a thief. She wondered if she would see him again and relapsed into the comforting thought that she would surely see Sir Andrew. And reminded herself that Roone had instructed her not to show openly her preference, which of course was correct, and she must warn Hester, even though Sir Andrew never seemed to notice.

Chapter 4

E ACH afternoon Stephanie waited in the dark drawing room to try to catch her aunt and persuade her that it would be safe and proper for two girls to walk the few blocks to the small Bedford Square and three times around and return home without the aggravating presence of the housekeeper. So far she had not succeeded. This time she was determined to advance the thought that two healthy girls should have more than the one walk a week on Sunday. She was gazing out disconsolately from the window seat, for in spite of the telling words she had found she had little hope of success, when a smart barouche drew up in front of No. 29. Amazed, she watched an elegant lady descend and fol low her footman up the steps. There was a knock, voices, a pause. Aunt Edita hurried into the room, patting the fat black curls.

"Lady Willoughby," grumbled the butler from the doorway.

A short lady who well filled out the simple lavender gown, which was matched by a plumed hat on top of brown hair, entered sedately. "Mrs Tinkham?" The voice was brisk. "So kind of you to receive me in this informal manner. But I felt I could not wait."

Aunt Edita advanced majestically, the wig quite overtopping the hat. "Lady Willoughby. It is a pleasure. Won't you sit down?"

They disposed themselves in facing armchairs. Stephanie, nearly hidden by the window draperies, was sure the lady had taken a complete inventory of the room and its mistress.

"I will come to the reason of my visit immediately," Lady Willoughby announced. "It is, of course, about Stephanie Langley, the granddaughter of my dear cousin General Nicholas Langley."

"Cousin?" Aunt Edita had grasped the important point.

"Oh, distant, but blood you know can be stretched quite far when a dear child is involved." The smile was small.

"So can ties by marriage," Aunt Edita snapped.

"But it's not quite the same thing, is it?" The lady waved a lavender-gloved hand as though dismissing the suggestion. "Yes. I have come to invite Stephanie to be my guest for the season. How fortunate it is just now commencing. I can give her a share in the gaieties and a real taste of London life, you know, which is desired for her."

"She has been my guest for four weeks," An edge crept into the flat voice. "I have begun to introduce her myself. We had to wait on gowns."

"Quite. But, do forgive me for speaking bluntly, our circles are quite—different, are they not? Oh, one does one's best," the brisk voice went on smoothly, "but her family feels her circle should be more on their own level."

"So kind, my lady. But I could not permit Stephanie to leave my home unless so instructed."

Stephanie's heart had jumped at the prospect of leaving, and now it sank.

"Of course. I have brought a letter from the general which authorizes just that." From a lavender reticule embroidered in black she produced a sheet of paper. "I'll read it. It says 'My dear Lady Willoughby. How delightful to hear from you. Your interest in Stephanie solves a problem for me. She is now residing with a Mrs Tinkham, on Eldon Street, a distant relation, by marriage, she claims, whom I only saw once some twenty years ago. She offered to sponsor Stephanie for a season, along with her own daughter. To my deep distress, I have gathered this is not happening in the fashion I wish. Yes, I agree I should have investigated her before allowing Stephanie to enter her household. But we old soldiers are not apt to think of fraud. I understand she has no entry into society nor has she spent properly the money I sent for Stephanie's maintenance and wardrobe. I have been contemplating coming to London, arduous as that would be for an elderly man, to remove Stephanie myself. But you offer me the perfect solution. Kindly call on this Mrs Tinkham and take away Stephanie and her belongings to your own home for the remainder of the season and introduce her as seems best to you. I also understand a considerable amount of the sum I sent remains unspent. It is repugnant to talk of money, but pray be good enough to inform Mrs Tinkham that it should be handed over to you, with an accounting, or to my lawyer who will call if she refuses you. I trust all to your good judgment. And, believe me, dear Lady Willoughby, I am in your debt for this rescue and take pleasure in subscribing myself your grateful servant.' "

Aunt Edita let out a sound meant to be a snort but it was wavering. "I never heard of such a thing. Of course I refuse. And I would never permit Stephanie to leave without my own dear Hester."

"Then I will take her also. Your motherly feeling is quite understandable." Lady Willoughby continued to smile a little, but there was no yielding in the brown eyes. "Why not summon the girls so we may tell them of the change in their lives? Or would you prefer to await the visit of the General's lawyer?"

"I do not wish to stand in my daughter's way," Aunt Edita executed a swift retreat. "I can see the advantages."

"Very well. The girls are at hand?"

"Oh, yes." Stephanie burst from the window seat.

"The dear child is so countrified she likes to sit at the window afternoons and watch the street." The titter faltered.

"I am surprised she is not out with your daughter and

a maid," Lady Willoughby observed thoughtfully. "So you, my dear, are Stephanie. I am your Cousin Doria."

Stephanie crossed and dipped a neat curtsey before she took the outstretched hand. The brown eyes were merry, now, and the face so friendly she could not help but laugh a little.

"Good," said Lady Willoughby. "We will be friends. So it is all settled, Mrs Tinkham? Stephanie, go and inform Hester and pack your things. I am sure you can do all that in the very few minutes it will take Mrs Tinkham to discuss the subjects that remain. We will go in my barouche and get a hackney for the boxes."

Stephanie sped to the stairs. She was excited and vastly impressed, for she had never realized a lady could be ruthless and still look kind. It took nearly five minutes to persuade Hester it was true and her mother would not descend that evening and drag her back to Eldon Street, and only ten more—how fortunate they had so little Stephanie pointed out gaily—to pack their boxes, don cloaks and bonnets, and hurry downstairs. Lady Willoughby's look of horror as she saw their garb and Aunt Edita's bridle as she saw the look made Stephanie choke back a giggle. Hester was a little teary and frightened as her mother waved her away, but after one look at Lady Willoughby she made her dip and gave the first happy smile Stephanie had seen on the thin face.

She must remember her manners, Stephanie told herself, and crossed to Mrs Tinkham, still rigid in the high-backed chair, and made a tiny curtsey. "Thank you for what you have done for me, ma'am," she said clearly and thought that adequately non-commital. The black head bent a little as the girls followed Lady Willoughby from the room.

Riding in the barouche was a new delight, for not only were the crowded streets full of fresh sights but the streets themselves improved as they went west. Lady Willoughby, alternately appalled and amused at their ignorance, answered their questions about people and vehicles they passed and named the streets and squares and promised they could go sightseeing once their clothes were in order. Her home, off Portman Square, was not a mansion, like some they had seen, but larger than the house they had quitted and seemed quite magnificent. Lady Willoughby conducted them herself to their rooms at the back of the second floor, told them to unpack and appear for sherry, and an early dinner, at seven in the yellow saloon, and left them with a bright looking second maid named Rose who would look after them.

"Stephanie!" gasped Hester, dropping into a chair, and looking around at the white woodwork and white wall paper printed with little bouquets of flowers, "what has happened to us? Isn't this beautiful? But how did it happen?"

"I don't entirely understand," Stephanie admitted, watching Hester with new interest. She had seemed only an unobtrusive figure, meekly obedient, before. Now there was a new light in the blue eyes and a touch of color in the cheeks and with her hair washed perhaps with a touch of lemon juice to lighten its blondness, she could be quite pretty. Above all, she would be a companion in this new world. She told what she had heard, omitting the matter of the monies, and pushed her to her own room to help Rose unpack.

Lady Willoughby was waiting for them in a small saloon with white paper flocked in yellow and yellow silk draperies at the windows. Beginning by informing them again they were to call her Cousin Doria, she chatted of the latest news of the Prince Regent, and an Italian soprano she thought vastly overrated, and asked a few delicate questions which she did not pursue. At dinner she lured the girls into talking of their schools. Back in the saloon she became more practical. "Now, my dears, I will inform you of what lies ahead. First you must be properly gowned—give those cloaks and bonnets to Rose immediately—and tomorrow we will begin on that. I am not taking you to the most fashionable modistes, for that would not be suitable. I must tell you now that there is no chance of your receiving vouchers for Almack's, though of course I know the patronesses. To be brutally frank, you neither of you have the pretensions or fortunes to appeal to those ladies or interest those who attend, and you are neither of you, I take it, on the hunt for wealthy husbands and social positions."

Stephanie put down her coffee cup on the little white table beside her. "You are right, ma'am. All I would like, would be most happy to do, is to have a glimpse of London and society, at a lower level, so as to gratify Grandfather and Mother and then return to Dorset. I believe Hester feels the same way."

"Yes," whispered Hester, "though, though, at the end . . ."

"We will consider the end when that time comes," Cousin Doria reassured her. "And you will not be at a lower level, dear Stephanie. There are a multitude of balls, routs, ridottos, breakfasts, festivities, which are frequented by all of society and to which the accolade of Almack's is not at all needed. Your grandfather will be quite satisfied. But does he mean you to find a husband? Does either of you have some gentleman on whom your heart is set?"

Sir Andrew's dazzling countenance flashed into Stephanie's mind, but while she was sure her heart was lost to him there was no chance his would be to her and she and Hester said a firm no.

"It is well to know these things ahead of time," Cousin Doria remarked comfortably. "Your dancing may be a little rusty so you will have some lessons. We will plan your wardrobes together, and enjoy it thoroughly." She smiled at them warmly. "I must tell you I am pleased with you both as pretty-behaved young ladies. When you have your gowns I will take you calling and to whatever festivities have appeal. In fact, I must confess I am delighted to have you with me as an excuse to be more frivolous than in the recent past, and I am convinced we will enjoy ourselves mightily."

"You are so kind," Stephanie burst out. "I do not understand, but, dear ma'am, we are most grateful for your—your interest. We will endeavor to do as you wish in all things."

"I know you will. Now, though it is early, run along to bed to recruit your strength for tomorrow." She beamed as they curtseyed and waved them away.

For a few minutes they speculated and marveled

and vowed to sustain each other and separated. But once in bed Stephanie found she could not sleep and got up and went to the door, wondering if the library could be on this floor so she could find a dull tome. But the hall was dimly lighted and all the doors closed and she decided she did not dare to go below, and was glad she had for she heard Cousin Doria laugh and the deep tones of a man joining in. She went back to bed wondering a little and telling herself it was none of her concern. It was as well she did not venture below, for all three persons who would have been involved would have been slightly disconcerted.

Over the tea table the man she knew as Roone was smiling at his hostess. "We did not have time to talk when I brought you the letter and instructions, dear Doria, and we have opinions to share. It was not difficult to locate a retired general named Langley. He has an agreeable small seat called Laneleet below Shaftesbury. He's a lively and delightful gentleman, sadly crippled with rheumatism, and openly devoted to his granddaughter. He was enraged at my report on Mrs Tinkham but his condition forbade the first action that came to his mind, which was to journey to London and use his horsewhip in spite of his age and her sex. When he calmed down he and his pretty and sensible daughter-in-law agreed to all I proposed. I enjoyed the night I spent with them particularly as it developed he and my grandfather had served together. He was touchingly grateful at my suggestion you take over Stephanie—he believes he knew your mother slightly —and all is in your hands. And I also am most grateful, for the girls could not be in better, though I am somewhat taken aback to learn you have two instead of one."

"But that is sensible, Esham, for though this Hester seems a retiring little thing it will be easier for Stephanie if she has a friend at her side. How agreeable it is you liked the family."

"Indeed, yes. But how fared you with the abominable Mrs Tinkham?"

"Excessively well, by threatening obliquely. The general's letter, with the mention of the lawyer, carried the day, and she disgorged a substantial sum which is not, I am sure, accurate, for the accounting she scribbled was obviously more fancy than fact. When she mentioned her daughter I thought of Stephanie entering a different world alone and pointed out that Hester would meet more eligible young men under my guidance than under her own but would only appeal if properly gowned. She'd like to get the girl out of the way and I suspicion there has been some hanky panky over her husband's will. Reluctantly she disgorged a sum that is nearly adequate. So I can see they are both outfitted in high, but not too high, style."

"Carry on as far as it goes and then send the bills to me. Send your household bills also, for I wish you to come out of this well, for you are being most kind." He drank some tea. "I told the general his sum would be adequate, which it will in part, for Stephanie, but the whole thing must bring some easement to you."

"Just to escape the household expenses will do that, dear Esham. I have a sufficiency, but one does run short at times." Her brown eyes twinkled at him. "And I will be pleased to have such a good excuse to frequent various affairs to a greater degree."

"Coming too rare, my dear. You have admirers aplenty to escort you."

"So kind of you to notice, but sometimes one likes variety. But I am devoured by curiosity. What has impelled you to take an interest in the girl?"

He looked down at his teacup then gave her a wide look that said nothing. "Frankly, I do not know. I encountered her first in unusual circumstances." His mouth quirked in a smile at the memory, and being urged, recounted the ride into town. "I felt sorry for her, when I heard how she was circumstanced, mildly interested by her very differences from the usual young lady, and thought I had forgotten her. But I encountered her again and found I had not, and that I liked her. Then I saw her at a fourth-rate gambling house and knew it would not do. The unspeakable Mrs Tinkham had probably taken her there in the first place in the hope that Stephanie, being a country chit, would believe this was the society she was expected to frequent and perhaps attract a suitor. That Stephanie was not deceived was an added attraction."

"But you have known so many girls of all types, even some of the most top-lofty have tried to engage your interest, for so many years." She frowned a little in puzzlement. "She is pretty and lively but she is not stylish, though she can be made more so, and she does not seem at all your type."

"I have no type," he told her lightly. "Yes, she has no town bronze, but she will acquire a sufficiency. Perhaps the explanation lies in a remnant of chivalry, concern for a damsel in distress, and boredom with the usual social round and the beauties themselves."

"But you have never been in the petticoat line." It was almost an accusation. "It is high time you were."

"True, but I am not now, I assure you, or likely to be." He gave her an engaging smile.

"But we will see you occasionally, I trust. Does the girl like you?"

"That was one attraction, Doria, and she seems to for myself alone, for she only knows me as Mr Roone. I find that oddly gratifying. And so I thank you again for falling in with my plans."

He rose and kissed her cheek and left. As he walked to his house he laughed. Doria liked to know all, but she did not know, and would not, that one chief reason for his taking up the cause of Stephanie was her friend Sir Andrew and what he had said of Lord Maleby and his errands.

It was the fifth afternoon, and since two appropriate dresses had arrived Cousin Doria suggested the girls might like to take a stroll to Bond Street to look at the shops. Rose, who was to be their abigail, was equally excited, and though she walked properly behind them, kept exclaiming and muttering she had never seen the like of the shops and the people until Stephanie, who knew that was not the thing, had to tell her to keep quiet. Rose did not take that amiss, but then Stephanie had to look around to make sure she was following them and not gawking at some ladies in a landaulet or some shop window filled with bright bonnets.

They had halted themselves to examine a display of gloves and reticules when Stephanie, glancing up, saw a face above her reflected in the glass. Her heart stopped a moment before she whirled and held out her hand. "Sir Andrew!"

"It really is you, Miss Langley!" He snatched off his hat and seized her hand, his face alight. "I could not be sure. You look so different!"

"How kind of you, for I know the difference is an improvement." She could not help laughing a little. "You remember Miss Tinkham. How goes it with you?"

"Poorly, Miss Langley, since I have not seen you these past days. You have not been to Mrs Riffton's," he added sadly.

"No. We have changed our address, both of us." She was sure she showed how happy she was to see him but did not care. And Hester was gazing raptly at him. "Come, walk a way with us and I will tell you," and she marched them both to the outer edge of the pavement. "You are still with Lord Maleby?" she asked, to give herself a bit of time.

"Oh yes, running errands for him, doing his letters, nothing has changed. But you . . . ?"

Discreetly pruned, she recounted their move to Lady Willoughby's, mentioning the direction. He nodded solemnly. "That is splendid. Much more your line of country. May I be permitted to call?"

Cousin Doria could not object to this lovely young man, and Stephanie assured him they would be happy to have him appear. A group of passersby having separated Hester a little, she looked up. "Have you been doing any searching again?" she whispered. How could she have lost him from her thoughts these past days?

He shook his head. The sunlight brought out the tan that remained on his face from his army days and made the eyes even more blue and the hair more golden. "Not really. Just one thing that I did not care for and had to do alone. But I must have been mad to involve you at all. I am covered with shame. Do forgive me. I just did not know what to do."

"You did quite right," she assured him enthusiastically. "And you must again, if something arises. It is your duty to follow orders from your superior and my duty, as we agreed, to help in any way I can. Pray call on me at any time."

"A true daughter of a soldier," he murmured. "I deeply hope I'll never be called on again for any such action, but I will remember you, I promise, for I am sure I could never carry out any such enterprise alone." His expression became troubled at the thought.

"Oh, you could," she told him stoutly, "but I hope nothing arises, though I so enjoyed the adventure. Where is Hester? We are at the end of the street and must return."

"And I must get on with my errand. I am off bounds a little here, but I could not resist a stroll on Bond Street. How happy, how very happy I am, Miss Langley, that I succumbed to the temptation, for I was quite in despair at losing you and too intimidated by Mrs Tinkham to question her. She is not really your aunt?"

"Not at all. A most distant relative by marriage only. Hester is quite different."

"I already know that." He smiled at the approaching Hester, which almost stopped her in her tracks. "Then, with your permission, I will call. Again, I am most happy to have encountered you." He bowed and walked on and Stephanie had to pull at Hester's arm to get her to turn from watching him and speak sharply to Rose to stop staring.

On the walk home, with Hester moving as if in a trance and Rose, behind, reduced to incoherent mumblings, Stephanie came to remember Roone's warnings at Mrs Riffton's. She had been stirred to the bottom of her walking shoes, she acknowledged to herself, and made happy by Sir Andrew's evident delight at seeing her. But she must not let anyone read her heart, as Roone had said, for she had her pride as a Langley and as a properly behaved young lady of twenty, and one rule in the romances she had read was that a hopeless passion must never be revealed. But if only he would call, if only he would need her again, that would be the most for which she could hope.

So she was able to recount calmly the meeting to Cousin Doria over tea. "Seddon?" the lady asked. "I do not know the name. From Suffolk? That probably explains that. A baronet, army, now with Lord Maleby you say? Of course we will receive him when he calls. You also met him, Hester?"

Still starry-eyed, Hester could only gulp and nod.

"My maid was telling me that Rose was maundering about some gentleman who had spoken to you, and that you have risen vastly in her estimation, Stephanie, by being acquainted with him. Let us hope he calls soon."

Chapter 5

BUT Sir Andrew was pushed to the back of Stephanie's mind again by Cousin Doria's decision that they should attend a small ball. She had taken them to call on two of her friends, and they had sat demurely, spoken only when addressed, and passed teacups without a spill, and been praised as very properly behaved young ladies.

"Lady Mabel Davenant is the daughter of an Earl, as you can tell by her title, and good form," Cousin Doria informed them. "She does not care for some modern customs and is pretty high in the instep about people and the affairs she attends. It will be a good place for you to be first seen, and yet not overpowering for you. You must both remember to converse with any gentleman who invites you to promenade, or dance, with him, and appear to enjoy yourselves but not to an excessive degree. In your new gowns I will be pleased to introduce you."

Stephanie's gown was a primrose yellow with a band of seed pearls around the neck, puffed sleeves and flounce and simply cut, Hester's was pale blue with bands of a slightly darker shade. Cousin Doria presented them with the necessary long white gloves and white silk reticules. Since she wore her favorite lavender, this time in flowing satin, the three gowns complimented each other deliciously, she observed as they drove slowly toward Grosvenor Square. Stephanie was only slightly apprehensive about the coming evening for, after all, she had attended dances at neighbors' and county balls at Shaftesbury and Dorchester. But she could tell by the tight clutch on the reticule that Hester was in a panic. So she set herself to draw out Cousin Doria on the people they might meet, and since the lady's descriptions were always amusing the clenched hands gradually relaxed. By the time they reached their hostess, a stout lady of imposing mien, Hester was subdued but no longer frightened.

"Ah, Doria." Lady Mabel looked down a short nose. "So these are the gels you've taken under your wing. Well. Agreeable. Wish you luck."

"So kind of you to let me bring them," cooed Lady Willoughby. "Yes, very agreeable. Quite different from the usual run, you see. Refreshing." With a bright smile she nudged Stephanie away. "She was unusually kind," she whispered, "can be an iceberg. So you both will pass. And I see one, no, two gentlemen waiting for us there by the pillar."

The crowd was such that Stephanie did not see how she could recognize anyone, but she led them unerringly. A minute later she was saying briskly, "Stephanie, my love, may I make known to you Lord Airde? And Miss Tinkham, Lord Airde."

But Stephanie barely heard the words. She was looking into amused hazel eyes in an angular face with firm cheekbones and a wide mouth now slightly turned up at the corners. "Miss Langley." The dark brown head bent over her hand. She drew herself up. Was this another of his deceptions?

"My lord," she said sedately and made a small dip from which she was glad he raised her strongly for her knees felt a little weak. He bowed to Hester and turned to Lady Willoughby. "And, Doria, may I make known to you Sir Andrew Seddon, of the Seventh, but now attached here in London?"

Stephanie jerked around to see Sir Andrew in modest but correct evening garb bending over Lady Willoughby's hand and caught the startled flash on the lady's face as he straightened. "But I have heard of Sir Andrew." In anyone else it might have been a gush. "The girls told me of their encounter. I am so pleased to meet you."

"Knew you would be," Lord Airde observed with a touch of complacency, "and he's practically fresh to London. Doesn't know anyone, so be kind to him. Now may I take Miss Langley on this promenade?" Without waiting for assent he offered Stephanie his arm, and when she did not move, took her hand and placed it and walked her away.

"You're improving." Laughter lurked in his voice. "There wasn't a flutter. No one would have perceived, except myself of course, that you were surprised."

"Of course I'm surprised," she said indignantly. "Is this another of your impersonations, trades, whatever you call them? I should warn Cousin Doria you once said you are a thief."

"I never said that, my girl. You just assumed it because I allowed I had been looking for something and left in a hurry. I am surprised you assumed the worst. I must confess I really am a baron."

"Then why did you say your name was Roone? You have been deceiving me all along, and I do not take kindly to that, sir."

"Roone is my second name. I seldom use it. Most people call me Airde, from my title you see. My closest friends call me Esham. If you would care to use it I would be flattered."

"Certainly not! What is your game?"

"No game, Miss Langley. I told the truth. I hardly cared to use my own name in an, well, unusual situation or in a place like Mrs Riffton's."

"Indeed?" Her irritation gave way to curiosity. "So I was correct in holding it a trumpery and vulgar place. Why did you go?"

"To see it for myself. And now I am bent on rescuing your Sir Andrew."

She knew he glanced down at her and that she blushed. "That would be most kind," she murmured.

"I fear he is not of sufficient experience to—understand and manage."

"Oh, he isn't," he agreed flatly, "and he's too good a chap to be wasted. Now look around the room. You'll probably not see it again and it is one of the admired ballrooms. And smile when you make any comment to me. Have you been to balls before?"

"Of course." Her annoyance returned and she started to move away from him but was firmly drawn back by the solid arm beneath her hand. "I've been to dances in Dorset and county balls several times."

"Ah, Dorset. So you have learned how to behave at such. Laugh as if you are enjoying my company and look around."

She laughed at the non-committal face above her. "Never did a gentleman so order me around," she said provocatively.

"Perhaps they did not have sufficient courage." He bowed to someone by the wall. So she obeyed him again. It was indeed a magnificent room, she discovered, made to appear four times its already large size by full length mirrors set into all four walls, each surrounded by twining flowers and vines in gilded wood. There were two white marble fireplaces and long windows between the mirrors with white sofas in front of them. The reflections of the guests, the ladies in all hues and the gentlemen in dark evening dress or scarlet uniforms, made a bewildering array on every side.

"How does anyone find anyone?" she wondered. "It would be so easy to walk up to a figure and find it only an image."

"That is held to have been the idea of the lady who

had it so decorated," he told her solemnly. "It is alleged she adopted it from Versailles. But it is also alleged she did it to thoroughly confuse her not-bright husband as to whom she was dancing with, and when she was on the floor and when she wasn't."

"Did it work?" Stephanie asked gaily.

"Exceedingly well, from her point of view. He challenged the wrong man to a duel and was killed. So she married a much brighter man who threatened to have the mirrors painted black if she played any tricks on him. So she didn't."

She transferred her attention from the room to the people. There were a number of girls of her own age, she was glad to see, with dashing young men in attendance, and an even larger number of stately elderly ladies, many with towering plumes in their wigs, and men to match, some tubby, some massive, some thin and straight as if still on the parade ground. Would she ever know any faces, she wondered, and caught sight of two.

"There are Hester and Sir Andrew," she exclaimed. "They are attracting some attention and not aware of it." Hester was glowing a little as she chatted and Sir Andrew was the model of gallantry as he bent to listen.

Airde nodded. "I wish they could stay that way. Doria will be pleased to have caught such a non-pareil. Let us join them for a few minutes."

The prescribed stately pace of the promenade could not be altered and the two were on the opposite side of the room, but Airde took her out of the procession and halted by the window to wait for the other two. He complimented them on their high looks, which made both blush.

"I say, my lord," Seddon burst out but in a low voice, "this is the most beautiful room I've ever seen. And the people . . . I am forever in your debt for bringing me. And to have found Miss Langley and Miss Tinkham is almost beyond belief."

"So glad," Airde said lightly. "Thought you might enjoy something other than Mrs Riffton's. You'll not be going there again, I take it."

"But I have to." The expressive eyes clouded. "Lord Maleby so orders . . . every Friday, from nine to eleven."

"Great Jupiter! Why!" His surprise was evident.

"To pick up dispatches. I go there, leave my cloak and hat, move around the room, venture a little at roulette, leave. And when I go I find in the inner pocket of my cloak or even in the pocket of my jacket a sealed paper or packet. This I then take and leave at Lord Maleby's residence."

"But how exciting," Stephanie observed enviously.

"No, ma'am, just another errand, and expensive for me, which I regret, but Lord Maleby does not take that into account and I do not feel sufficiently at ease with him to mention it."

"Since you have to play," Airde suggested absent-mindedly, "put your counter where two lines cross and you might occasionally win enough to recoup your loss. But do you know what the papers are?"

"Oh, yes." Sir Andrew brightened. "They are notes from agents. I have written replies as my lord dictates. One may be about a French lugger hanging off Plymouth, or three men seen landing at Pevensey and disappearing inland, or an observation about activity at a French port. Lord Maleby says they are from secret people who work for him and send information he can use. My thanks to you, my lord, for the suggestion about the roulette." He gave a pleased chuckle. "It would be a most welcome change to win at all."

"So I hope. Can you identify any of the persons who might be bringing these messages?"

Sir Andrew shook his head. "No, sir, there are too many people in the room. It is always crowded and full of movement."

"Convenient. Are instructions to the agents returned somehow? Not by you, I take it."

"It is my impression that is done through Mr Philippe Meriney, a refugee and a co-worker on Maleby's staff, for he has said he attends the place on Tuesday evenings and dislikes it as I do."

"Obviously a successful arrangement. Come, sir, we must return these ladies to their Cousin Doria and be on our way. But may I propose a drive, two afternoons from now, to take tea in Richmond. The park is handsome." A sudden charming smile lightened the rather aquiline face as he offered his arm to Hester, who gave a little gasp as she accepted it and began to walk sedately at his side. Sir Andrew smiled so openly at Stephanie she could but reply in kind and listened with pleasure as he recounted how Lord Airde had found his lodgings and brought him tonight to see a totally different side of London.

The men bowed to Lady Willoughby, who was seated on a sofa, an older man at her side, as Airde said they were expected elsewhere and obtained permission for the tea at Richmond, bowed to the young ladies, and headed for their hostess.

"That is really a gorgeous young man," Lady Willoughby exclaimed, "and does not seem to know it. Several have inquired about him. He could become the rage, but I am sure Esham would guide him away from that for it nearly always ends in disaster. My dears, may I present Sir Charles Fortby who is not going to rise because he has a bad leg." She twinkled at them all. "And now here is Lady Mary with two young men who are eager to dance with you. Remember to return to me always."

The two young men were pleasant and danced well but Stephanie found that even the activities of a country dance were not so exciting as a slow promenade with Lord Airde. But she and Hester acquitted themselves gracefully, thanks to their lessons, and two more were waiting to take them into the next dance.

"You did very well, my loves," she approved as they drove home. "All those young men are quite eligible. Yes, I know you are going to say you are not seeking husbands, but you must know it never does a girl harm to be seen sought after by eligible young men. Nor," she added thoughtfully, "will it do you harm to be seen driving with Lord Airde and Sir Andrew."

They arrived at Montague Street in a dark blue phaeton that glowed rather than shone. Lord Airde led Stephanie to the box seat beside him. "Yes, I know," he remarked as he guided his grays toward the park, "you would rather be behind with Sir Andrew. But it seemed to me that Miss Tinkham, not being accustomed to phaetons, would feel more at ease now in the back seat, and then at ease in the front on the return."

"That is thoughtful of you, my lord," she agreed a little stiffly.

"Isn't it? Also, you know, by rights you belong up here in front with me, but no matter. How do you enjoy life with your Cousin Doria?"

Stephanie tried to refrain from unbecoming enthusiasm, but she could not remove the gaiety and excitement from her voice and face as she touched on all the delights she had never imagined. Her warmth did not seem to be excessive for from time to time he glanced down with an amused and approving look. Also, she noticed, he knew a great many of the people they passed in the park before they took the road to Richmond.

"Then I gather all is a success and you will retire to Dorset content with your London visit. Has Seddon said anything more to you about searching for papers?"

"When we met on Bond Street I managed to ask him so no one heard. He said he had had to do only one thing alone and had not cared for it. And . . he apologized for involving me, but I assured him I was ready at any time to do my duty."

"Bravo." The tone was dry. "Perhaps there will be no further orders."

"I hope not, for it does not seem to me fitting for a gentleman and an officer, is it sir?" She raised troubled eyes.

"No, it isn't. But one must obey orders, as he has

said. You are very fond of Sir Andrew?" he asked abruptly.

Stephanie looked down and folded her hands. "It would not be proper for me to feel, or admit, such an emotion," she said primly.

"Then I will rephrase my question. You enjoy his company?"

"Oh, yes." She glowed at the thought and gazed up at the quiet face above her. "He is so very kind and appreciative and thoughtful and enjoys everything so much and is so frank and open. And too unspoiled, I fear, for his own good. It makes me happy that you, who are so much older, are now his friend."

"Much older!" Surprise made him drop his hands and the grays shot forward. Quickly he brought them back to a trot. "What do you mean much older?" he demanded sharply.

"But you are." She was surprised in turn. "Much older, and of course wiser and more experienced, as I should have said. Cousin Doria has remarked that you are known as a Corinthian and an admired man of the town."

"How old is Seddon?"

"He once allowed he was twenty-four, and that he was brought up simply, with due care paid to duty and manners."

"Evident. The army has given him some experience, of a different kind. How old are you?"

She raised her chin. "That is not a question to ask a young lady," she rebuked him. "But since it is probably evident I am on the way to being put on the shelf, as Aunt Edita told me several times, I will admit I am twenty."

"An advanced age, to be sure. I will have you know, Miss Langley, that I am twenty-seven."

"No . . . I can hardly believe that!" Her eyes widened with shock. "You seem, er, much older. But," she added thoughtfully, "perhaps that is because of the years in the army and the life you have led in London."

"Undoubtedly." His voice was now neutral. "But I am happy you feel I am a proper guide for Sir Andrew."

"Oh, I do. You act so much older anyway it is quite intimidating at times."

"Indeed? Then I must ration those times. Here we are approaching the Rose and Crown where I have bespoke a table under the arbor."

She leaned forward and put a hand on his arm and looked up anxiously. It would never do to have him take a dislike to Sir Andrew because of anything she had said. "You will forgive my mistake, sir?" she pleaded. "I meant it as a compliment. In contrast to Sir Andrew, you see, and all as wholly admirable."

His glance was inscrutable. "You are forgiven. I can see how it came about. And remember never to touch the driver. It can be—distracting."

The Rose and Crown was long and half-timbered. Stephanie was sure it had been made to look more Tudor than it was in reality, but there was no denying its attractiveness. The phaeton was led away, after some admonitions by Lord Airde to the hostler on the care of the grays, and the party was guided to a table at the end of a rose-covered arbor in a garden at the back. Stephanie exclaimed at the flowers and the privacy, at which Lord Airde bowed, and she wondered how often and with whom he had used the place. A refreshing punch appeared· and then sandwiches and cakes, an appetizing concoction of scrambled eggs and chicken livers with herbs, and tea.

When they vowed they could eat no more Airde straightened. "In addition to the pleasure of your company, I confess I brought you here so we could talk openly. With your permission, I will go into the matter directly. Seddon," he half turned, "you are still under orders from Lord Maleby to seek for certain papers from time to time. As it happens, I am under similar orders from my superior. Yes, I know nothing much seems to have been done, but we move slowly in this country and usually in ways not visible."

Sir Andrew nodded. "I have wondered that nothing seems to happen, but could not question."

"Of course not. Now my proposal is that we combine forces, pool our knowledge, when we have any, and search together when instructed. Otherwise we will be in a contest with each other, and getting in each other's way. Our combined efforts might well be more successful than working alone. And no one need know we are being of assistance to each other. What say you, Seddon?"

The curved eyebrows creased a little. "That does indeed make good sense, my lord. I have felt very ignorant in the matter. That was why I enlisted Miss Langley, though I realized quickly it was not proper I was nearly desperate. You are so much more experienced than I am, sir, that I am happy to be guided by you. We are both soldiers and do our best for our country."

"Indeed we do. But I do not agree you were so wrong to ask the aid of Miss Langley for it is quite true that a young lady can wander around a house with no one questioning her. She was doing well, on her one venture."

Blushing at the allusion but disregarding it, Stephanie nodded quickly. "I am so glad. I am most eager to be of use. I can follow directions to a nicety."

"But is there nothing I can do?" pleaded Hester. "I do not know of what you are speaking, but on any enterprise I would be sunk in the depths if I could not take part." She gazed from one to the other appealingly.

"Of course you can," Sir Andrew assured her. "Let us see. You can keep watch, warn us of any danger approaching."

She clapped her hands. "I can cough, quite loudly, or scream that I have seen a mouse."

"Splendid," exclaimed Sir Andrew while Lord Airde laughed, "you will be our advance picket."

"And you and I, Seddon, will devise a means of communication. Your lodgings are not very convenient."

"But the best I can afford, sir," Sir Andrew answered with dignity.

"Quite. We will find something comparable. Now, have you any idea which men have access to dispatch boxes in your department?"

"Yes, sir. I made a list. There are only a few with

carte blanche. There is Lord Bevenham, but he had nothing but his own papers. There is a retired admiral who is seldom seen. And two other lords."

"Who are they?"

"Colesham and Ockhampton," Sir Andrew answered slowly. "All papers are quite well guarded. We aides are only given the papers we need at the time."

"Then all we can do is wait on events. I think it is as well we are to act in concert, and with such charming assistants," and he gave a slight bow.

"We will hope we never need them," Sir Andrew hesitated, then went on, "I have wondered why he gave me your house, sir, and without your name, for me to search, and for something you obviously could not have."

"I, too, have wondered," Airde agreed, "and I can only think it is because we have taken a violent dislike to each other, have indeed since we first met. Who are the other aides?"

"One is Henry Bart who works on figures of all kinds and has been there fifteen years. The other I mentioned, Philippe Meriney. He was sent to Lord Maleby by a French friend, he once said, and does errands and writes letters as I do. He is ardent in his hatred of Napoleon and the revolution that preceded his rise to power, for in that turbulence Meriney's family lost their estates and had to flee and had great difficulties existing here."

"As happened to so many. Lord Maleby is also loud against the French."

"Yes. Sometimes they become quite violent in their

consultations, which are in French. Lord Maleby maintains his agents are useful in the information they suply about events in France and agents landed here."

"Who are in contact with traitors, no doubt," Stephanie injected hotly. "Some men can always be bought, grandfather says, and may be found anywhere."

"I am afraid your grandfather is right, Miss Langley, but let us put them from our mind. Miss Tinkham, will you do me the favor of joining me on the box seat as we return? Tell me first what is your favorite topic of conversation?"

"The country, sir," she cried in a rush. "Anything about the country I dearly love to hear."

"Why is that?" he asked gently.

"It is so beautiful and has such appeal. I once visited a friend in Hampshire for a week. It was wonderful, trees, meadows, streams, gardens, and all the darling animals. When I returned I could talk of nothing else, so my mother shut me up quickly. And she never let me go anywhere again. But I still remember . . ." Her voice trailed away.

The three watched her with compassion, for never had she said so many words at once or shown such emotion. "But your father?" Stephanie asked. "Surely he . . ."

"My father was dead by then," the light voice rushed on. "He died three years ago. Oh, we loved each other so much. From the time I was young he would take me on walks, entertain me, take me to his office, for I should learn about woods and his business so I could watch over my share of his wealth. My mother did not care for the bond between us but could not oppose him, but she has kept the money he left me, to come at eighteen, and has never permitted me to visit any friends."

Suddenly the round eyes flooded and she burst into tears, shoulders bowed, head in her hands. Stephanie jumped up and knelt beside the girl, one hand outstretched to receive a handkerchief from Sir Andrew. "There, there," she soothed, "of course the memory makes you cry."

Hester sniffed, took the handkerchief and dried her eyes. "Forgive me," she faltered. "I know one should not indulge oneself in public. But it is that you are so kind to me. No one has been kind since my father, and for a moment I could not bear to think of him."

"Of course." Stephanie rose and brought the girl up beside her. "We will go and wash your face and you will feel right in a moment and another cup of tea will set you up entirely."

Between the tea and the promise she would hear about a pet rabbit and, yes, a pony, Hester was laughing happily as she walked to the phaeton.

"A sad tale," Sir Andrew said thoughtfully, "but I can believe it all."

"I also," Stephanie agreed warmly. "No wonder she so enjoys our present life." Smiling at each other they followed.

Encouraged by words such as "lambing time," "herb garden," "meadowland" that floated back from the front seat where Airde was answering a flow of questions, Stephanie and Sir Andrew fell into descriptions and discussions of their own homes. Differences and likenesses, and a partiality for fly fishing, made their talk lively. Sir Andrew even condoned, since she was a delicately nurtured female, her confession that she remained far from the kill when out fox hunting, which she joined for the exhilaration of riding across country.

Lord Airde glanced back. "You must stop that line of talk," he admonished. "The thought of hunting upsets Miss Tinkham. Her affections extend to even the most predatory of foxes." They could hear him adding to the slight figure at his side, "No, no, often the fox outwits us, and if one doesn't, why think of the lambs and chickens that have been rescued."

Why, he's being very kind, thought Stephanie in some surprise, and, after a mischievous glance at Sir Andrew, she spoke of dogs.

The sun and the light breeze had given both girls color and a slight disarray and they were looking particularly pretty as they were set down in Montague Street. "Delightful girls," Sir Andrew observed thoughtfully as they drove away.

"Yes," Airde agreed, "unusual. Now, I will leave you at your lodgings to change. You will return to dine with me and after that we will find a further glimpse of London life. No, do not thank me. It adds to my consequence to be seen with a new figure of distinction."

After a light dinner of only two removes Airde announced they would stop first by a club for another glass of port before going on to two small affairs. There he watched with approval Sir Andrew's composure when introduced to rather terrifying old gentlemen and his impassive courtesy while one expounded for five minutes on the things Wellington had done wrong and right on the Peninsula. They strolled on toward two chairs, Sir Andrew never examining his surroundings or evincing undue interest, and arrived as a short, white-haired man caught sight of them.

"Airde, come hear my extraordinary adventure," he cried.

"A pleasure." Airde bowed. "May I order you a port with ours and present Sir Andrew Seddon, Lord Bevenham?" Beside him he felt Sir Andrew stiffen as he bowed in turn.

"Yes, yes, delighted, thank'ee. It is this." He faced Airde, who stepped slightly in front of Sir Andrew. "One night, last week it was, I was walking home carrying a fat packet of papers. Was just past my corner on Weymouth Street. A figure, all I saw, came from an alley, struck the back of my head, stunned me. Knocked me out for a bit, no real damage, old head's too hard, ha, ha, caught my shoulders, lowered me down. Then took papers, seals, watch and carried me to me own steps. Was coming to, told you my head's hard, when footman looked out a window, noticed me. I said it was a footpad, too many around you know, and glad to get off so easy. Now, mind you, the odd thing is this. Next evening, dusk, footman answers knock on front door. And on the sill is packet of papers and inside watch, seals, everything. Almost gladder to have papers, they were plans for new rose garden and belvedere. Now, what do you think of all that? I never heard the like."

"Perhaps our footpads are turning philanthropic," Airde offered lightly. "It is in truth a remarkable tale, my lord, and I congratulate you on your escape."

"As I do myself. Nothing like a hard head. There's Lithgow, must go tell him." He bobbed his head and began pushing his way through the room. Airde eyed his companion thoughtfully. The young man's hand was steady and his face without expression. Airde lifted his glass. "Congratulations to you, Seddon. Was it like that?"

"Yes, my lord." The answer was soft.

"Well, drink up, man. We're walking to our next stop so you can tell me."

In silence they turned left from St. James's Street. "Well?" prompted Airde after a moment.

"It was as he described, sir." Seddon spoke without emotion. "His office is down the hall from Lord Maleby's rooms, and he often carries papers home and follows the same route. Lord Maleby told me to get what Lord Bevenham carried however I could, saying he never notices young men and would not recognize me. I did not care for the idea but knew I could do it and not hurt the old gentleman. I did hit him, but not hard, believe me, sir. Then, as I was leaving, I looked back and saw him lying on the ground and could not bear that he should be a prey to any passing footpad or stray person. So I took his belongings to keep them safe and carried him to his own steps so he would be found quickly. Lord Maleby was not at all pleased that the papers were so, well, personal, and told me to discard them, though he did commend my success. It seemed to me the only right thing to do was to restore everything. So I did. But I deeply regret the incident and hope it will never be known."

Airde glanced at the now troubled face. How much the man had revealed by that description . . . "You did exactly the right thing," he tossed off casually. "Never fear. It will not be known."

"Thank you, sir. I am greatly relieved. And happy to see that the old gentleman suffered no ill effects and acquired a good story to tell. My conscience has bothered me."

Airde stifled an exclamation at the noun. "What would you most prefer to do, if given free choice?"

"Go back to my regiment, of course." Seddon was surprised there should be any question. "I know the men need me, few take as much interest as I do. I—I enjoy the army, and serving England."

"Good man," and Airde turned the talk to Mrs Wills, at whose house they would stop briefly for a concert (to which no one was supposed to listen) and meet a few people. "I am looking for a young man for Miss Tinkham and I have one in mind if I can run into him. Devoted to his sheep in Sussex, where he has a pleasant estate quite large enough to support all the animals with which Miss Tinkham is so erroneously enamored. I think they would approve of each other."

His conscience reassured, Seddon turned almost lighthearted and brought out some pretty speeches when introduced to a variety of ladies. They went on to a rout where, in an aura of approval, both men were gaily welcomed.

"I can't thank you enough, my lord," Seddon said earnestly as he descended at his lodgings. "It has been a memorable evening. My mother would be gratified that I have remembered a sufficiency of her instruc-. tions. It makes up for a great deal."

Airde wondered at that but did not pursue the remark. "Delighted you accompanied me. And since we are to be partners, perhaps you might take to dropping the 'my lord' and call me Airde."

There was a hesitation. "It does not seem fitting, sir."

· "What? Too old? Nonsense. Good night." The hackney was gone.

Chapter 6

THE gentleman sought by Lord Airde proved to be Mr Henry Fendell, come upon in the taproom of the Three Crowns tossing dice, left hand against the right, for, he explained, he had nothing better to do at the moment and could not leave the city because of a matter of wool and sheep. In answer to Airde's blunt question he stated with some warmth that not only was his interest not fixed on any female but he had not encountered in two weeks a girl with whom it was worth conversing or who had any interest beyond her clothes, her beaux, and the latest gossip. Promising to alter that unhappy situation, Airde took him off the next day to Lady Willoughby's. Fendell was welcomed, place made for him at an angle from Hester's. Remembering his coaching, he soon introduced the words "lambs" into conversation, at which Hester leaned forward eagerly.

Airde gave a glint of a smile at the other two. "That will do, I trust," he said complacently. "It was beholden of me to provide a fourth for your company as I am going into the country for a few days."

"I'll have you know, sir," Stephanie put on a touch of hauteur, "that Miss Tinkham and I are not solely dependent on you and Sir Andrew for masculine company, pleasant as yours is," she added hastily.

"That relieves me of one care," he drawled in a manner that made her wish to hit him. "So, I leave you in good hands, many of them," and he turned back to his hostess. But when he came to say goodby to Stephanie he looked quite serious, eyes intent. "I trust you will use your good sense and not join Seddon in any—adventure while I am gone. Whatever may arise can await my return. Do you so persuade him." That sounded like an order, and Stephanie tossed her head a little and told him she always used her good sense. He raised his eyebrows in a way she found offensive, and left.

Perhaps it was fortunate, she reflected, that no orders for any untoward activity had come to Sir Andrew, for Lord Airde had sounded very decisive, and Sir Andrew could also be decisive, and she would be reluctant to be caught between them. Mr Fendell proved as eager to act as escort as Hester was to listen to his account of country activities, so he frequently made a fourth, and enjoyed comparing notes about Suffolk and Sussex. He envied Sir Andrew his army experiences, explaining he would have joined up but there was no one to run the place after his father died, and would have pressed for tales of camps and fighting, but Sir Andrew turned him off politely, which Stephanie regretted but Hester approved.

A possible problem had occasionally troubled Stephanie, and one day after tea, when Hester had gone up to shorten a petticoat, she broached it. "Dear ma'am," she began, "perchance I am borrowing trouble, but one thought keeps returning. It is what of that dreadful Mrs Tinkham. It is hard to believe she will not attempt to get her claws into Hester at some point. What could we do then?"

Lady Willoughby picked up the last cake, took a nibble, put her head on one side and looked serious. "The same thought has come to me, love. She is a most horrid creature. And avaricious. I fear that when she sees some way to make use of our Hester she will not hesitate. The girl is nearly nineteen, but unmarried. Mrs Tinkham would be considered her guardian, to guide her future."

"That is what I fear," Stephanie said quickly. "There must be something we can do to save Hester."

"I have thought on it and I have a notion that now, since you have the same fear, I will follow. If only Esham were here—he is so wise and always knows what to do. But I'll not wait on him. He takes off on private trips and there is no telling when he will return. Yes, you encourage me, and no, I'll not tell you in case

I have to think of something else. But somehow we will stand by to repel boarders," and she gave Stephanie a wide smile.

Having been comparatively successful with one question Stephanie asked another that had been nagging at her. "Is it true that Lord Airde is a soldier? Sir Andrew said something . . ."

The brown eyes looked at her in surprise. "But of course. I thought everyone knew. Three years on the Peninsula, first in the lines, for he chose the foot, most oddly, over the cavalry, and was twice wounded leading his men. Then Wellington refused to let him go and get shot at again and put him on his staff. A most exceptional officer, Airde was held, cool in any crisis. He was off on some mission and was wounded once more and then sent home firmly to the Foreign Office where he is highly esteemed."

"Thank you," Stephanie managed, overwhelmed by the tribute.

Three nights later Lady Willoughby's party attended an affair at Lady Donnington's. There was to be an edifying lecture on life in the Holy Land at the time of Abraham followed by dancing. They were going, she explained, not for whatever inspiration might be derived from the lecture, to which few would listen, but friends would be there and Lady Donnington was good *ton*. Sir Andrew and Fendell had accepted with enthusiasm the invitation to act as escorts.

Lady Donnington evidently had no illusions about the competing attractions of her evening's entertainment. A front room was partly filled with three rows of uncomfortable gilt chairs and a subdued cleric in one corner who had at least been provided with a comfortable divan on which to await his auditors. Telling the four to wait, Lady Willoughby went over and spoke to him in such a kindly fashion that he brightened visibly and thanked her.

"I told him his talk sounded fascinating and that when I have completed my obligations, which he quite understood, I would slip in and listen. It never does any harm, you know, to be kind to all clergy, for one never knows when one may need one, does one?" She waved a hand and dismissed the thought. "Now let us go and mingle and see who we find."

After strolling around the ballroom, containing as yet no musicians, and discovering a good number of friends, Lady Willoughby preempted a sofa where she promptly was flanked by two gentlemen. Seddon urged the two girls and Fendell through the long windows on to a long balcony that ran the length of the wing.

"It will be cooler," he pointed out, "and we will enjoy the dancing more if we are refreshed."

"By Jove, yes," approved Fendell, and leaning over the railing exclaimed again, "By Jove. Funny thing. I was just telling Miss Tinkham of my orchards and how one prunes apples and pears in a different fashion and there is a pear tree down in the garden. Will you accompany me, Miss Tinkham, so I may demonstrate how it is done? There are stairs back there which will take us to the paths and quite enough light from the torches for you to see."

"I would enjoy that," Hester agreed quite merrily.

The two departed and Seddon looked after them, then at Stephanie. "He is a good chap, of course," he allowed and then leaned down, his eyes twinkling, "but, tell me now, does she really enjoy his discourses?"

Inevitably she twinkled back. "A lady always enjoys a gentleman's discourse. At least she appears to do so on the surface."

"What lowering information, for who knows what thoughts may be mingling beneath that surface. I am intimidated. May I fetch you a glass of punch and give you time to order your thoughts?"

"Mine are always in good order in your company, sir," Stephanie laughed, "for I genuinely enjoy your converse," and wondered if she had been too forward, for his face lighted up with pleasure. "Yes, punch would be welcome."

"Then I will bring it to you. I have no need to examine my thoughts when in your company, for they are always happy." He stepped back through the window quickly.

Gratified by his remark, Stephanie looked over the garden and could discern two figures on a path at the back. There was nothing else of interest to see so she strolled along the narrow balcony, passing the windows of the ballroom, hung with a pale green silk that billowed and moved pleasingly, and coming on three others, dimly lighted with curtains apart. With no hesitation at all, she peered within.

It was a lady's sitting room, for the furniture was in the delicate fashion of the last Louis, with a chaise longue, a few chairs and, beside the window, a fragile desk. On the corner of the desk, almost beside the window, stood a black box, open, stuffed with papers. Almost without thought, she stepped over the sill, scooped up the papers and retreated to the balcony, bending to read as she turned them over.

Simultaneously two sounds jerked her upright. One was firm footsteps approaching her on the balcony. The other was a high treble shriek from within the room. The steps quickened. Sir Andrew appeared on the opposite side of the window, punch glass in hand.

"Miss Langley," he said sharply. "What have you there?"

"Papers. From a box. I thought they might be . . . but they are only love letters."

Carefully he set the glass on the wide railing of the balcony and seized the papers. "See," she gasped. "One says 'My own beloved darling' and another in a different hand starts 'Moon of my Delight.' Oh . . ." Her voice trailed away as another shriek burst out in the room.

"Stay here," ordered Sir Andrew and stepped through the window, one hand holding the papers behind him. Stephanie peered around the edge of the window.

Lady Donnington was standing in the center of the room, eyes on the gaping box, hands clutching her bosom, mouth open to scream again. Sir Andrew in a second had bent slightly sideways and deposited the papers on the floor by the desk and strode to the lady and caught her clasped hands.

"My lady, quiet, don't scream. You will attract attention." His low voice was commanding.

"Oh, yes." Black eyes flew to his face. "But my

letters," and her voice threatened to rise again. "They are gone."

"Where were they?" He was guiding her toward the desk.

"There." She snatched her hands away and pointed to the box. "I am ruined."

"No, no," he soothed her. "A breeze perhaps. They must have been blown out."

"Oh, find them." Her ample bosom was heaving and she gazed beseechingly at him.

"Why, yes. That is simple. See, ma'am, they had fallen on the floor." He stepped, bent, gathered the letters together and offered them to her. She snatched them, riffled a few and looked up with flushed gratitude. "Yes. You are right. Oh, kind sir, put them in the box for me. I am shaking." Hands clasped again, eyes anxious, she watched him. "It is folly to keep them, but they are such a comfort when one is over— over thirty. I was reading them again to raise my spirits before going out . . . to meet people, you see, knowing I will not see one of . . . them . . . I was called away and I forgot."

"So easy," said Sir Andrew gently, pity for a moment on his face, for the lady was far beyond thirty. "Where does the box go, ma'am?"

"In my secret cupboard, of course. I am still shaking. Walk to that panel painted with plums and press the lower left one." As he did the panel door swung open and he placed the box in the cavity and closed the panel. "Oh," she gasped again. "Young sir, you are most kind. I will always remember you with gratitude. My husband, you know. Now, I must . . ."

"Return to your guests, my lady. Compose yourself on the way. Act as if nothing had happened, as indeed nothing has."

"Would you come with me, sustain me?" she asked, extending one hand.

He shook his head. "That would be unwise. It might cause questions. You have been absent long enough. You do not need me. Raise your head. Remember you came to speak to one of the maids."

She nodded, gave him a long look, put up her head, turned with a swish of green taffeta and marched through the open doorway. Sir Andrew stepped back through the open window.

"Oh." Stephanie clutched his arm with both hands. "How clever you are. You said just the right things."

"Why, you are kind, but no." He shook his head. "I just said what was obviously sensible. But I confess I was nervous, so many possibilities . . . May I share that punch? Now it is over I am overcome at my temerity."

At his insistence she took two sips herself and he solemnly turned the glass and drank where her lips had been, a pleasing gesture. So, quite calmly, they strolled along the balcony but on the way had to stop, for they caught each other's eye and burst out laughing.

"You are wicked, Miss Langley," Sir Andrew finally managed. "I admire your enterprise, but never do such a thing again."

"I won't, I promise. I was quite terrified. But you rescued me so beautifully."

"Couldn't let her scream and bring people running.

We'd have been suspected of—anything, even if you appeared suddenly as chaperon."

"I am abashed. But I trust if I make any other error of any kind, you will be at hand again."

"It is where I would hope to be, Miss Langley, and not in case of error only." She was glad she did not have to reply to that and to hear that the pear tree, for the other two joined them suddenly, had not been pruned properly, but Mr Fendell would say nothing about it to his hostess because gardeners were so touchy.

Dancing had begun when they entered the ballroom though only a few were on the floor so Stephanie and Sir Andrew joined the slowly perambulating double line. They had circled once when Stephanie spotted an approaching couple. "Oh," she gasped, tightening her fingers on his arm. "Lady Donnington is approaching. If she notices me I will have to remind her of you."

"Of course," he told her calmly, tightening his arm so her hand pressed against his side for a moment. "Have no fear."

Lady Donnington was moving rather majestically at the side of a large thickset man whose graying hair was arranged in a careful row of curls across a wide forehead. The lady's glance was sweeping around the room, keeping track of her party as a hostess should, while she inclined her head a little toward her partner's flow of talk. Stephanie felt the glance rest on her and her companion and then, in a few paces, the four were somehow face to face. Since the older pair halted the younger had to also.

"Ah," Lady Donnington smiled at Stephanie. "Miss Langley, is it not, with dear Lady Willoughby?"

Stephanie curtsyed. "So kind of you to remember, my lady. And perhaps you also remember Sir Andrew Seddon, who accompanied us."

The handsome face and fine dark eyes gazed at Sir Andrew, who bowed. "Why, of course," the social voice said in a way that meant it was not to be believed. "Mis Langley, here is Lord Maleby . . . my lord, Sir Andrew Seddon."

The heavy man extended a hand toward Stephanie. "Miss Langley? By any chance are you a relation of General Langley?"

"I have that honor," Stephanie allowed, perforce extending her own hand and finding it engulfed in two hard ones.

"Granddaughter, no doubt. I should have guessed . . ." Lord Maleby beamed and made a very small bow. "A pleasure indeed, Miss Langley. Ah, Seddon." The nod was condescending. "I did not know you had acquaintances who could bring you to this delightful affair. I hope," he swung back, "to see you again, Miss Langley. Perhaps you will favor me with a dance?" He bent his head in almost ducal fashion and moved off beside a chattering Lady Donnington.

"That came off very well," Stephanie murmured as they paced forward.

"Knew it would," Sir Andrew whispered comfortably. "I never believe in anticipating trouble. So often it never occurs."

What a sensible way to feel, she thought, and smiled

at a young man who was eagerly asking for the next dance.

After an exceptionally delicious supper the four were waiting for the musicians to return when Sir Andrew was accosted by a thin-faced dark-eyed young man. "Seddon! A pleasure to see you away from that office."

Sir Andrew looked pleased himself and presented Mr Philippe Meriney, his colleague, who attached himself to them. He proved a lively conversationalist, his intensity and vivacity making all he said of appeal. Hester was pleased when he asked her to dance.

"He's a refugee," Sir Andrew told Stephanie as they followed. "His father had a title and estates in Normandy. They escaped here but have had a thin time. He does not mind saying he loves France and hates Napoleon. Oh, blast," and he halted as Lord Maleby approached, come, he proclaimed, for the dance Stephanie had promised. It turned out he preferred to promenade and he spent the time telling her of his place in Sussex, his estate in France, and his close friendship with the Prince Regent, adding two anecdotes to support his claim. While she listened with an attention she hoped was duly flattering, Stephanie was wondering what Airde would think of the incident with Lady Donnington and could hardly wait to tell him.

That opportunity came a few days later when he arrived at teatime. Hester was visiting the zoo with Mr Fendell, chaperoned by Rose, so Stephanie was sitting to one side while Lady Willoughby entertained three of her favorite friends. Lord Airde was welcomed, but after one cup of tea Lady Willoughby waved him away.

"Take Stephanie to the library. We have some delicious on-dits to discuss and they are not for her ears." At that the ladies tittered self-consciously as Airde bowed and said "Servant, ma'am," and Stephanie rose and made a dip.

The library was a small room made dim by dark paneling and a wall of leather-bound books. Stephanie tripped quickly to the chairs by the window. Glancing at her dancing eyes, gleaming curls and light dress he slowly smiled. "You light up the room, Miss Langley. I can see you are in fine form. You have been enjoying yourself. Any further news or activity involving our friend Sir Andrew?"

Glee filled her and she gave a little bounce, quite forgetting his compliment. "Not of the kind you mean, sir, but something else did happen."

Long legs stretched out, he was relaxed in his chair and she thought he looked tanned and a little weary. "You have been on a long trip, sir?" she inquired, momentarily diverted.

"To Plymouth, to straighten out a tangle with each government office trying to thwart the others. Regretfully I fear my solutions will not endure for long. But what did happen at the ball?"

"You are right, it was at a ball, Lady Donnington's. It was not a real adventure, and Sir Andrew was wonderful." She smiled widely at the quiet face opposite and plunged merrily into the whole account. At the end she burst out laughing. "I do wish you had been there to enjoy it with us."

To her shock, he sprang to his feet, took a few steps and came back to loom over her, his face ablaze with an anger that darkened his hazel eyes and set his face in hard lines.

"You little fool." His ice-cold voice held fury. "Is this how you behave when I am absent? You haven't the brain of a peahen nor the discretion of an oyster. You said you took the letters on impulse. Don't you know how to control your so-called impulses? You could have been caught, disgraced, created a scandal of vast dimensions, ruined young Seddon as well as Lady Donnington and yourself. Thank heaven for his presence of mind. He evidently belongs in the diplomatic service as much as in the army. Oh," he flung away and paced again. "I have no patience with such a feather-headed girl."

At the outset she had cowered, put her hands to her face, frightened by his anger, but her spirit rose. "You have no need to have patience, my lord," she cried hotly. "What I do is no concern of yours. There was no harm done. I had thought you would be as amused as we were. We have told no one."

"You are both too innocent to be allowed off a leading string," he grated. "You don't understand what might have happened." He stood over her again, seized her wrists, jerked her to her feet and gave her a shake. "Don't you ever set one toe out of line again, my girl. Yes, you had it in mind to help Seddon, but that is no excuse to act like a ninnyhammer. You're not to think of giving him your so-called help again." He let her go and stepped back, his eyes still darkened.

"You have no right to mistreat me or to order me around." Her voice shook which increased her anger.

"You are outrageous and domineering and rude beyond belief. I'll do as I wish, or as Sir Andrew wishes." She glared back at him. No one had given her a shake except her nurse. Never had she been spoken to in such a fashion. It was not soothing to realize that much of what he said was just.

He gave her a long look and strode away and she found it more comfortable to sit so plopped down in her chair. He returned in a moment, all anger wiped from his face, regarded her a moment, and took his own chair.

"I should not have spoken so, Miss Langley, or allowed my feelings physical expression—though," he said evenly, and there was again a flash in his eyes, "you deserved it all. You are too inexperienced to understand and too high-spirited for your own good. Please believe me when I say what you did was most —unwise. And please believe I have only your own good at heart."

She looked squarely at him, wishing she could hit him, show her outrage in some violent fashion, but realized that would also be most unwise. She looked down. "Yes, my lord," she said in a small voice. "I will remember and try to improve."

"Good." He leaned back and crossed one leg. "I will, of course, say nothing to Seddon, who behaved most admirably. Did anything else occur at the ball?"

Surprise held her, for evidently he could master his fury as quickly as it rose, and she needed to move her mind back. "Not much sir. I met Lord Maleby. He was with Lady Donnington. I reminded her that Sir

Andrew had come with us and he and she looked as if they had never seen each other before." That should reassure this odious man.

"Of course. What thought you of Maleby?"

"An unpleasant man," she said emphatically. "So— so heavy in form and manner and as self-important as a turkey. He claimed to have known my grandfather, but I doubt it."

"So do I. It was quick-witted of him to connect the name. He's an upstart. His father paid handsomely for a title and a mansion in Hampstead and he has added a holding in Sussex. He got his post by toadying to the Prince Regent. No one cares for him, but he is clever and has power. Who else?" Airde was conversing as if nothing had occurred between them, which was a challenge to do likewise.

"A confrère of Sir Andrew, a Philippe Meriney, dark and emotional but subservient to Lord Maleby."

"I have heard of him. No other news but that you and Miss Tinkham have had a lively time with all those gentlemen you assured me were at hand? Then I must be leaving. Our interview has been most instructive, Miss Langley. Good day." And he was gone.

Stephanie lingered, thinking of all the things she should have said to that arrogant man when she had the chance but impressed in spite of herself by the force he had shown, and slowly returned to find Lady Willoughby alone and to receive morsels of the on-dits, which she did not really understand. She was glad they so occupied the lady that no questions about Airde were asked.

Chapter 7

FOR four days Lord Airde and Sir Andrew did not appear. Stephanie and Hester agreed it was peculiar but fortunate, for they had several invitations to drive and to attend the opera with various young men and now stood up for every dance at balls. Then, at tea, a note in firm black writing was brought to Lady Willoughby. She laid it down and looked at the two girls with surprise.

"It is from Airde. He informs me he will come for you both tomorrow at four to take you to call on Lady Diana Inverskaid. He will bring Sir Andrew. It quite takes my breath away."

"Why, dear ma'am?" Anything that startled Cousin

Doria must be unusual to a degree. "Who is the lady?"

Lady Willoughby fortified herself with half a cup of tea. "She is one of the *grandes dames* of the world, my love, now retired from it. She never sees anyone unless she summons them. Callers are turned away. She scorns society, says it is shabby and has lost its style and spirit. I do not understand . . ."

The girls looked at each other and indulged in a giggle, which brought a frown. "It is not a laughing matter and giggles are unseemly," she told them sternly. "You must dress and behave with the utmost circumspection. She knows everyone, or knows of them, and somehow all that goes on. If she should say you are ill-mannered or insipid the world would know it. But it is most strange, for she never tolerates young people. But, of course," she added thoughtfully, "she is a great-aunt of Airde and they have had an affection for each other, it is said, over the years. But . . ." she eyed them. "Let us look at your gowns now and see if aught is needed for tomorrow."

After looking, she determined new hats were essential, so the following morning was spent on the purchase of a demure chip straw for Hester and a green modified polk with just one small plume on the left for Stephanie. New gloves were then required and new reticules, and by the time the girls were gowned and waiting they were about to develop the set of nerves they had been warned against. Airde would bring his barouche, Lady Willoughby told them, for one did not call on Lady Diana in a phaeton.

Arriving at four on the dot, he kissed Lady Willoughby, whispered in her ear, told the girls they were looking in high bloom and ushered them to the carriage where Sir Andrew stood.

"Doria has probably told you something of Lady Diana and put you in a quake," Airde began briskly. "There is no need. She is, when she wishes to be, highly entertaining. She also prides herself on her singularity, but that has nothing to do with you except you must show surprise at nothing. And only speak when spoken to."

The mansion on Chandos Street looked as if it had been built when the Conqueror was at work on the Tower. Tall, square, flat faced, it could equally well withstand a siege, Stephanie felt, and shivered and then slowed her steps; she would not be hurried by anyone. Airde noticed and gave a low chuckle. "Not going to be intimidated, eh? You are right . . ." and slowed his steps to match.

Two footmen bowed them through thick lofty doors, two more bowed at the foot of the stairs that led to the next floor. A butler marched in front of them as if carrying a rod of office and ushered them into a high-ceilinged room, part library, part salon, and large enough for a ball. An immense black-stone fireplace, bearing a shield with at least sixteen quarterings picked out in gold and blazing colors, mounted to the ceiling at the far end. Branching candlesticks, all alight, marched cheek by jowl along the mantelpiece. Toward this they were guided and then halted in front of an object of glowing pink.

"Bring them nearer, Blodgett, you fool," commanded

a deep voice. "I can't see 'em at this distance. Bring them chairs. Bring more candles."

Obediently the four moved forward again. The pink object was a sedan chair lined in silk of a paler shade, holding piles of cushions. Amid them sat a square-shouldered lady, also in pink, with a mass of white curls and extremely bright black eyes.

"Esham," said the commanding voice, while soft sounds behind them indicated there was unseen activity, "don't stand there like a dolt. Present your friends."

"Dear Aunt Di." Airde moved easily to the chair, raised one hand and kissed it. "I never presume to bring my friends nearer for fear you will order them removed immediately and it would save time if they are closer to the door."

"Impudence. I only did that once. Now?"

At Airde's smooth voice Stephanie advanced, curtsied, and made way for the others.

"They are perfectly presentable, Esham," approved the lady. "And I must say your friend is a fine figure of a man." Sir Andrew blushed and contrived a small bow. "Never saw a better," the lady approved again and gave a deep laugh. "There, sit down. Tea is coming. Esham, fix these dratted cushions. I wish to sit up straight."

She straightened by herself as Airde adjusted pillows and a cup of tea was bowed into her hand by Blodgett. "Nice of you young things to come to see an old lady. You," she nodded at Stephanie, "your name again and where you come from? Langley from

Dorset? Must be related to General Nick, one of the most charming subalterns I ever knew."

"He is still most charming," Stephanie said clearly, forgetting not to speak.

"He would be." Lady Di nodded again. "Good bones and head and figure—and charm. You. Tinkham from the City? Father was a merchant, wood as I remember, and an honest man. You . . ." and she beamed at Sir Andrew who blushed again.

"He is wonderful, Esham," she exclaimed. "I haven't seen a man in fifty years who blushed. You are in the army, of course, sir, and where before that? Suffolk? Seddon?" She shook her head and eyed him again. "You have a look . . ."

"My mother was a Noreton from Lincolnshire," Sir Andrew said composedly.

Lady Di nodded. "Of course. Saw it. You are detached to London? Not for long, I hope, for your sake. On whose staff? Maleby? A low-born come-lately who would never have reached any position but for his father's money and his own fat friend." She finished her tea with a flourish and accepted a fresh cup from Blodgett. "Now, go away, Esham, and talk to Prue as you always do about my health and ask her what I need and I will tell you if she is right or wrong. I am going to indulge in the favorite pastime of us all and talk about myself to these polite young people. If I don't they will ache with curiosity and never know the right of it."

"At your orders, dear aunt," murmured Airde and departed.

"Now." The teacup was thrust into a waiting hand and vanished. She sat up even straighter—it was evident she was quite tall—and pounded one pillow at her side which made another slip out of place. Stephanie sprang up and pulled it back where it belonged and pushed another. The bony face with a high-arched nose, high cheekbones and strong chin nodded approval. "Got it right the first time, child. Some never can. Go sit down. All of you take more tea and scones, young need to eat. There . . . You are wondering why the sedan chair and I will tell you." Her voice had a vibrancy that did not go at all with age.

"First. I use it because I like it—now. Used to prefer my howdah, though they do shake you up unmercifully. Second. No one else in London has one in their home. Third. Because I decided I'd done enough walking in my life and would not do any more. Gad, yes. Had to live up to my name. Wish I could measure all the miles—over moors, up mountains and glens after inoffensive deer and birds because my dear Archie liked to hunt. Then, same reason, tracking tigers, wild boars, chasing snow leopards we never found over mountains far too high, wading through rice paddies far too wet or across dusty plains. Didn't even stop when we came back from India. Archie said I was the best walker he knew." She paused and looked far away. "Then I lost Archie. No need to walk any more so I stopped. Got this up from the cellar. You're wondering why pink. Archie liked the color. Always hated it myself. It's said to be becoming with white hair but I never believed that. And there we are."

Stephanie let out a breath. "Thank you, ma'am, for telling us. It is fascinating. Think of all you have seen and done. Oh, how I envy you."

"Tigers," whispered Hester.

"I'd like to go to India," Sir Andrew said thoughtfully.

An expression of amusement lighted the craggy face. "You are nice children. Esham, what did Prue say?"

"That you are stronger than most women of forty, dear aunt," his voice coming from behind them, "which I did not need her to tell me, for you never looked better. And that you need nothing."

"Quite right. Well, now I am retiring. Seldom waste more than ten minutes on people but see I have. Esham, you may bring your friends again, when I tell you. You may remain here as long as you like. Now fix the pillows again." She sat back in a half reclining position and clapped her hands. Four footmen appeared at the instant with two long poles they thrust into gilded loops on each side of the chair and lifted it. She leaned forward, waved, and was borne away. More tea and scones appeared on a table by the window and the door was shut in silence.

"Let us move over there," suggested Airde, "it is more cheerful than in front of that monstrosity of a fireplace. You are comfortable? May I say you did well, my friends. Now let us talk. This is the only place I could think of where we would be neither observed nor overheard."

"You asked *her* if you could bring us?" Stephanie gasped.

"Assuredly. She and I understand each other."

"But is it all true, what she said?" Stephanie was still dazed by the pictures conjured up by Lady Diana.

"Indeed, yes, and much more. She can walk quite well, really, but she slipped on some ice and broke her hip and limps a little and does not want anyone to see that. So she satisfies her love of the bizarre. But, Seddon," he shifted in his chair, "you look worn and weary. What has happened?"

Stephanie turned. Sir Andrew did look tired and, somehow, worried. The poor man, she thought. He needs someone to look out for him—not in the army of course—but out of it, someone to whom he could talk and who would take care of him.

He rubbed his hands over his face, a gesture unlike him, and when he looked at them his eyes were troubled. "Yes. Not much sleep. But don't know if I should tell you."

"Come on, man. Remember we are going to help each other. What is it?"

Sir Andrew sighed. "Glad to tell you, really." He paused and sighed again. "Lord Ockhampton died, you know, suddenly, three days ago. Word came to Lord Maleby in the late afternoon. Instantly he sent Meriney and me, with two portmanteaux, with orders to bring in all the papers we could find. Things were in confusion at the Ockhampton house, the lady put down to rest, a daughter having hysterics, servants running around. We told the butler, only one keeping his head, who had sent us and he just showed us into the library and left us. We dumped everything we found, except one box of ancient documents that obviously belong in a muniment room, into our bags and departed. Lord Maleby was waiting for us, took us into a room with a large table and told us to spread out all we had and go through everything."

"Still looking for papers with a red circle?" Airde asked.

"So he said, or anything pertaining to affairs of to-day. Each of us was to go over everything and stay until we had. He did have coffee and sandwiches brought to us around midnight. We were still there when he arrived next morning. Three generations of papers we had, never saw so many. But we found nothing for which we had been told to search. Maleby was not pleased. Called us stupid oafs and other things and looked through some himself. Then we had to take them immediately back to the house. A man of affairs was there by then and highly annoyed at our removing the papers and at the order that sent us. We went back to the office and were put to work and not freed until late evening."

"A long stint and none of it proper," Airde sympathized. "This Meriney, you said he does the same work as you?"

"Yes, sir. He's very pleasant, though he goes into the *alts* whenever Boney is mentioned. We never discuss what we do."

"Wise. But what else? I can tell there is more."

Sir Andrew looked up from his hands. "This morning Lord Maleby summoned me. He said the last suspect is Lord Colesham. I am ordered to go through his papers, quickly and successfully. I must find the missing orders, papers, there. And," he looked down again, "I have no idea how to go about it."

"A pity Maleby has the Regent's favor," Airde said absently. "So it's Colesham now." He jumped up, walked to the far end and returned to his chair. "We'll do it together. Don't be so downhearted, man. There's a big affair coming up. Doria will have had an invitation; I'll urge her to accept. I know his heir, Parling, aimable chap, devoted to his pleasures. I'll get in the house, discover the lay of the land. We will go together to the ball."

"And we can help," Stephanie said decisively. "You will need ladies to cover your purpose, to stand guard, oh, anything."

"I cannot endanger you," Sir Andrew muttered.

Stephanie thought fleetingly of all Airde had said about the Lady Donnington episode, but surely this was quite different. "Nonsense. If there is a traitor he must be uncovered and Hester and I will be most useful."

"You know," Airde spoke as if thinking out loud, "I am not convinced those papers we both seek are the whole story, or if, indeed, they exist. There must be something underneath. But what? We can only plow ahead. . . . Come, I'm taking you all to your homes."

Reluctantly Stephanie rose at what sounded like an order and looked around the room once more. It would be something to · remember, so would the whole afternoon. She hoped she would see Lady Diana again. And now there was the ball ahead. She heard Sir Andrew saying, "Kind of you, sir, but I must go back to the

office. I slipped out and Meriney is covering for me.
I can't leave until dismissed."

"Very well. But then to bed, or you'll be no good
for anything. Ladies, the carriage waits." He had them
out in five minutes.

Stephanie felt a little weary herself, but realized she
must explain more to Hester than the girl had been told
so far. Hester took it all calmly, only saying that Sir
Andrew and Lord Airde must be helped, and obeyed
in everything.

Chapter 8

ON the edge of Hampstead, the Colesham mansion was another of the large houses set in its own grounds. To convey them all Lord Airde brought his larger coach since it could hold five without excessive crowding.

"You know the Colesham place, Doria, but the young ladies might care to learn something of it before they arrive," Airde began as the coach moved down Montague Street. "It is quite grandiose, built by the previous Earl from profits from India. On the first floor above the ground—the stairway is overwhelming, I warn you—are the usual public rooms, saloons, dining rooms, all that. The bedrooms, where you ladies will leave your cloaks, are on the next floor and so are the earl's study and library. The ballroom takes up most of the top floor."

"I can't see why we need to be given a map of the place," Cousin Doria said a little tartly. "It is like many others."

"Oh, it is," Airde agreed, "but you might care to have it all in mind in case you wish to retire at any point to repair your gown or have a coze with a friend. Young Parling drank until he was well above himself at White's a few nights ago and I saw him home. He insisted on showing me the place and telling me of the affairs he would hold when it is his. Though he seems a little reluctant to acquire the wife he would need to do it all quite up to the nines."

"I thought he was casting lures at the oldest Wendle girl," exclaimed Cousin Doria, and the two launched into witty speculations which the others could not follow.

In spite of the four tiers of windows, well lighted, and torches set around the coping of the roof, the Colesham mansion looked formidable. Stephanie wondered how anyone would dare set a foot out of line on the premises, much less search for papers, but told herself to trust to the Roone part of Airde to accomplish everything with ease. The earl and the countess were formidable also, beaky and gray-haired, but as cordial as their station permitted. It was a comfort to see an occasional face she could recognize, and she was gratified when Lady Donnington gave the group a slight bow.

"Parling told me this used to be all dark," Airde

remarked, nodding at the white and glitter of the ballroom. "Present countess had it painted white over violent objections of her mother-in-law. It caused quite a rift in the family, for it was against tradition. Also, removed all the tartan hangings." He glanced around. "It's much better now," he approved. "Come, Stephanie, this is a waltz and since you've nothing to do with Almack's there's nothing to stop our enjoying it."

Since the waltz was still thought fast by the dowagers of Dorset, Stephanie had a moment of doubt that she could perform adequately, for she had had only one lesson, but Airde's look was imperious so she allowed his arm to go around her and was surprised at how natural and comfortable it felt. She was light on her feet, had picked up a sufficiency, and Airde's guidance was so firm that in five minutes she was floating in the most delightful of dances.

"It is my plan," he began, once assured his partner presented no problems, "for us to wait until the crush is just before its peak. No one will be wandering to the floor below at that time. There are two rooms Seddon and I should go over, a study next to Colesham's bedroom and a library beyond. He and I will go down quite openly, as though to brush our hair, and trust we will have the time we need."

"Hester and I will go down just before you, to mend a flounce," Stephanie went on firmly, "and station ourselves, one to a room, to keep watch of any approaching person and warn you."

Airde started to frown. "I had not planned on such. You should not be involved."

"Then you should have so planned, in spite of that order you gave me so vigorously, for you cannot have your head in a désk drawer or in a cabinet and be watching the door," she told him with a touch of exasperation at his lack of foresight.

He gave a quick grin. "Still looking for adventure, eh? I hope you don't find it. You waltz quite well, by the way. Very well, we'll give you ten minutes warning so you can get ready. Remember the two rooms are to the front of the house, the rooms for you ladies toward the rear."

They exchanged partners and Stephanie was pleased there was sufficient demand for her hand to keep her dancing steadily. But she could not forget her coming role and kept watching Airde, who seemed to her excessively popular with ladies of all ages, for his signal. When it came it was between dances. She and Hester had been returned to where Cousin Doria sat on a white satin-covered sofa, flirting expertly with two delighted middle-aged gentlemen at once. Airde strolled up beside them, complimented them on their dresses, glanced at the doorway, and strolled away. Stephanie caught Cousin Doria's eye, lifted her dress a fraction, pointed to it and the door, and Cousin Doria nodded, never missing a syllable in her chiding of one man as being an outrageous flirt. Sedately Stephanie and Hester walked around the edge of the room, and making their way between groups of elegantly gowned ladies and gentlemen, gained the stairs and the rooms for the ladies below.

Fortunately the rooms were empty, even of an attendant maid, and it was the absent maid that gave Stephanie her idea. "We cannot stand around as we are and look anything but suspicious. We must have a disguise. Here." She snatched up two delicate towels from the washstand in the corner and held them in place with a hairpin from the dresser. "There. That looks like a cap. Fix mine." She looked around again and found two towels large enough to tie around their waists. "If we are maids we must do something." From a cupboard she pulled out two small cloths. "Now we have an excuse to be anywhere. But . . . " She snatched up a pot of rouge and rubbed two round spots on each cheek. "That is our disguise too," and sped out the door with Hester following.

The rooms they sought opened into each other and also into the hall. Hester she stationed in the study, a room that held a massive desk, chairs, a long bookcase. "We are dusting," she said a little breathlessly, "at least if any one enters. Books always need dusting on the tops. I'm going to the library."

This was larger, with books along the walls and also tiny *objets d'art* on tables, on the mantle, in a glass-fronted étagère. She had just lifted a jade figure of an old man when Hester arrived. "Someone is coming. The steps are not Sir Andrew's."

"Go to that bookcase." Stephanie nodded across the room.

Steps stopped in the doorway. A side glance showed two elderly gentleman surveying the room through their glasses. Oblivious, Stephanie lifted another figurine.

"Umph. Maids. Well, the Coleshams keep a well-run household but maids cleaning during a ball is excessive," a thin voice said acidly.

"Oh, I agree. But one must admire the motive. We can't talk here. Let us go to the conservatory," and the men moved away.

The next steps were familiar. "Seddon, you take the study," Airde murmured from the doorway. "I'll take this. Fortunate Lady Donnington didn't turn around and spot us. Take the desk first. If you have time try out the paneling. Good lord! Maids dusting."

"Yes, my lord," Stephanie managed to keep the gurgle in a low key. "Hester, go back to the study but stay near the door."

Hester ran to the next room. Without another glance Airde strode to a towering secretary with drawers below bookshelves. Seddon had followed Hester. Stephanie did not dare watch Airde so she picked up another bibelot. She heard drawers opening and closing. From the study came a thud and at the same moment the towering figure of Lord Colesham came up the hall and stopped at the study door. "Here, sir, what are you doing at my desk?" he exploded.

"As I passed the door, sir, I saw the drawer on the floor and stepped in to replace it." Sir Andrew's voice had only a slight tremor.

"Nonsense. Don't believe you. What's that? A maid? Did you . . ."

"No, sir," Hester gasped. "Never touched the desk, sir."

"Get out. No business here anyway. You. You're

Seddon aren't you? Under Maleby. You're spying.
Looking for something. I'll have you discharged.
Cashiered from the army, prosecuted. What *were* you
doing here?"

"Nothing, sir," Sir Andrew answered woodenly.

"Don't believe you. Someone bribed you. I'll have
my men lock you up now. Tomorrow I'll take care you
get your deserts."

"Why, Lord Colesham, are you shouting at my escort?" Lady Donnington—by stepping back Stephanie
could just glimpse her—stood in the doorway.

"Your escort, ma'am?" Lord Colesham lowered his
voice.

"Sir Andrew kindly escorted me down the stairs
while I went to repair the edge of my skirt. He was
waiting for me."

"Humph, ma'am. You know him then?"

"Certainly. A most gallant officer, sir. Sir Andrew,
will you escort me back to the ballroom? It is a delightful affair, sir."

As Stephanie stepped back she saw Sir Andrew walk
to the doorway, very calmly, and offer his arm. She
stepped further back and was caught in two strong
arms and swung around so her back was to the door
and Airde was not only holding her but kissing her
lightly.

"You, sir," barked Lord Colesham. "What are you
doing?" . . . .

"Obviously kissing one of your pretty maids," Airde
answered, lifting his head.

"Oh, Airde, it's you. Why?"

"I might say I wished a change from the formal ladies above, sir. I saw her dusting and felt I should relieve her of that onerous duty. I admire the good taste of whoever chooses your staff."

"Housekeeper. But surprised at you."

"I always believe in seizing an opportunity," Airde told him airily.

There came a chuckle. "You always did in war, I heard, so you're carrying the practice over into peace? Very sound. I'll take a look at her later myself. Well, I'll leave you to it, but not too long, mind you. Must keep up appearances, eh?" There was another chuckle as Airde bent his head and kissed her again, harder this time.

"You haven't been kissed much, have you, love?" he whispered.

"How do you know?" Stephanie gasped, being short of breath.

"I know," he murmured. Then, more loudly, "He's gone. Hurry now. Take off that outfit and that rouge, it isn't becoming, makes you look like a punchinello. I'll wait for you."

"It wasn't put on to be becoming," she said indignantly. "It's a disguise.' As the arms dropped she felt for a moment bereft and then, at a push, ran for the door.

Hester, towels discarded, was scrubbing her face with one of them. Stephanie was glad she had an excuse to scrub too, for as she recalled Airde's mouth on hers and the way his arms had tightened she knew the color in her cheeks would equal the rouge she was removing, and dabbed on some cold water.

"You didn't get all that color off," he observed as they joined him at the stairs.

"I scrubbed too hard," Stephanie faltered, trusting he would believe that, but he had turned to Hester.

"That was quick thinking, bringing in Lady Donnington," he told her. "Did you tell her he had lost his way? Of course she'd stand by him." He turned back. "You had better dance with me again, Miss Langley, to give that color time to fade." They went up the stairs and he thrust a faintly blushing Hester at a nearby rather bemused young man.

"It's my belief," he said in Stephanie's ear as he guided her, in what she was happy to find was a waltz, to one side of the room, "that Maleby has made up this whole ploy. I know papers are lost or overlooked on occasion, but," and he frowned a moment, "I don't see why he should be acting as if it were all as important as Trafalgar and involve Seddon as he has. That was a near thing tonight, and could have brought ruin. But," and he looked down and smiled so engagingly Stephanie almost blushed again, "you both were —invaluable. And a very pleasant excuse you gave me for being where I was."

"I'm glad you enjoyed it, sir," she said saucily. "Any time. We aim to oblige." Then she feared she had been too forward.

"Why, you little minx," he laughed. "What an invitation."

"From a parlormaid," she countered swiftly. "Do not forget I was in disguise."

"So I will hope to find you in disguise again soon,"

he said, with another laugh. The laugh chilled her, for obviously those kisses had meant nothing to him.

"And, yes, there's Seddon," he went on as if talking to himself. "I'll have to look out for him."

"Pray do," Stephanie interrupted eagerly. "He needs that. He thinks everyone is as honorable as he is. And look how he needed rescuing just now."

"He should have learned in the army not to trust people." Airde gave her an odd look. "I can see how he arouses protective feelings, he's as guileless as a baby chicken." He shook his head, and, the dance ending, returned her briskly to Cousin Doria.

The coach had joined the long line clomping into town before Airde broke the silence. "Yes," he began as though continuing a conversation, "the girls deserve an attention. Doria, wake up. I'm talking about your protégées."

"I'm not asleep," she yawned delicately behind one hand, "just resting my eyes. I don't know why elderly gentlemen feel they have to dance twice as fast as young ones. To show they are better men, I suppose, or how far they are from the grave. It is very tiring. What were you saying? You girls needn't laugh; you'll find it's true, in time."

"I was saying I am taking Miss Langley and Miss Tinkham for a drive in the park tomorrow. I'll find someone to take your place, Seddon, know I'll have to. You'll be given a setdown for having no success."

"I'm sure I don't know why anyone should give Sir Andrew a setdown," Cousin Doria said with asperity. "He *is* a success, or almost. Lady Donnington can't say enough on his behalf and took him to two girls to meet and dance with. I'd not be surprised if she takes him up."

"You know we men aren't always appreciated by ladies as we deserve," Airde tossed over his shoulder as he left the coach to hand out three slightly bemused ladies.

True to his word, Lord Airde arrived in his phaeton accompanied by a blond, pleasant looking, impeccably dressed Lord Branborn, who took his place beside Hester in the rear seat. Airde talked of trivia until they reached the park, then glanced sideways at Stephanie.

"That's a new hat. Very becoming. It must be agreeable to be able to wear every color well."

"So you notice such things?" Stephanie was surprised. "One never knows if gentlemen do or not for compliments seem routine to most of them."

"I always notice, ma'am. I was so instructed by the first girl I loved. I must have been fifteen and she was married and an experienced twenty-three. She kindly did not laugh at me and gave me a deal of good advice on how to get on with ladies of all ages."

"Which you have used to advantage ever since," Stephanie murmured, returning his glance but demurely.

"Of course. Though I have added certain refinements. But as to Branborn, now. I thought a change from Fendell was indicated. Branborn is very respectable, third of the title, not in the petticoat line, welcome everywhere. He hasn't a feather to fly with and is too lazy to do anything about it."

"What could he do?" Behind her she heard the easy drawling voice holding Hester enthralled.

"Marry a rich wife, of course, probably a daughter of a cit who wants to buy a title into the family. He's fussy, though, refused two girls. Said he didn't like their faces and couldn't listen to their voices for more than five minutes. So he sits like a ripe pear on a branch, just waiting for the right mama with the right daughter to pluck him off."

"That's very unenterprising."

"It's exactly the right thing for him to do. He enjoys life on tick, for his creditors know it will happen some day, and the kindness of his friends." He turned his head. "You talking about Sussex, Branborn?"

"Rather. Found Miss Tinkham doesn't know it. Most beautiful county of all."

"Are you going to buy back your home when you can?"

"Of course. Though the price may be a bit steep. Present owners have fixed the roof and the stables. County getting to be too fashionable, though. Ainsworth's bought a place and Maleby did, though his is almost on the coast. Afraid others will follow. That puts up the price, you know."

"Perhaps not." Airde dropped the conversation as he moved his team smoothly out of the way of a mismanaged curricle and looked at Stephanie and grinned widely. "Have to laugh," he explained, "when I think of you and Miss Tinkham in that getup. You were bright as a button to think of it, and right about our needing lookouts. But I'm afraid poor Seddon is having a rough time with Maleby." His voice trailed away.

"What about your own time, when you said you were Roone and looking for something?" Stephanie asked suddenly. "You were wicked to gammon me so when you found me in your own room and pretended it wasn't."

"My dear girl, I was saving you from embarrassment. And I was looking for things, several times. Some elderly gentlemen are occasionally absent-minded and carry home papers they should not and forget to return them. I'm supposed to keep track of such, when we learn of it, and retrieve whatever is missing, and however I can. That's what I had been doing the evening you picked me up. Since I had found what I sought the incident was closed."

"I hope Lord Maleby will close this one and free Sir Andrew from those horrid orders," Stephanie said, and, feeling it would not be tactful to talk more of Sir Andrew, reverted to a subject of almost equal interest. "I did not realize until I heard it from Cousin Doria, that you had been a soldier. You do not seem very warlike, sir, except when you give orders."

"Oh, I'm not at all warlike," he admitted cheerfully. "Dear Doria is given to occasional exaggeration, you must remember."

"She said you were in the army three years and wounded three times."

"Her figures were right, for once, but the wounds were not very serious. I dislike violence, Miss Langley, and will go to some lengths to avoid it."

At that she nodded approvingly. "My grandfather has said that good officers in war use their intelligence.

It is brains that succeed more often than brawn is one of his favorite sayings."

"And you follow his precept on occasion." His amusement pleased her. "Except when adventure beckons."

"But you know that adventures need brains too," she told him loftily, but was pleased again when he laughed.

Chapter 9

"Everything seems to commence at teatime," Stephanie remarked idly as the footman handed Lady Willoughby a note.

"Of course," Lady Willoughby told her absently, "that is the proper occasion for notes and calls and no one would know where they were without them."

"The person is waiting below, my lady," intoned the footman as the note was opened.

"What?" She stared at the neat writing. "This asks if Lady Willoughby and Miss Tinkham will be good enough to receive Mr Arthur Coburn. But I do not know anyone named Coburn."

"I do," Hester admitted faintly. "A merchant. My

father knew him. He came to the house once or twice."

"What can he want?" Stephanie wondered.

"I cannot guess," Hester faltered, "but it would be disrespectful if I did not receive him. But I can do so alone, ma'am, if you would prefer."

"By no means. Since you feel it is your duty to receive him of course we will remain with you. Very well, Paul, you may show up Mr Coburn."

The man who was shown in was round of face and round of body, not very tall, dressed in neat dark brown. He bowed over Lady Willoughby's hand, not very deeply because of his waistline, nodded to Stephanie, and beamed at Hester. "You are most kind to receive me, ma'am," he said in a sharp but flat voice, "and, dear Miss Tinkham, it is a pleasure to see you again. I bring you affectionate greetings from your dear mother."

"How kind," gasped Hester as Lady Willoughby asked him to sit down, which he did in the largest chair. Looking around the room, one hand feeling the cloth of the covering of the chair, he nodded. "I knew it. When Mrs Tinkham gave me the street and number I knew I would find it a bang-up establishment, with everything of good quality."

"So kind," Lady Willoughby echoed Hester faintly.

"No, no, ma'am. The truth. I can judge. In cloth, you see. I know the good from the shoddy." He beamed again, his sharp little eyes darting from the dresses to the rug to the draperies.

"How does my mother?" Hester asked with an effort.

"Splendidly, but of course she is sadly lonely without her dear daughter. But we hope to change that soon."

"Oh?" Lady Willoughby asked, after a glance at Hester. "How is that?"

"Since you ask, ma'am, I'll come to the point directly, though I had planned to come up to it gradual, like a bee to a flower, so to speak. It is this way." He leaned back and made himself comfortable. "I've a good business and I'm well considered in the trade. Miss Tinkham can vouch for that, for her dear father, a most highly esteemed man, favored me with his friendship. In fact, I'm a warm man, as we say up north. Two wives I've had, and after my early years, they never wanted for anything. But six months ago my second, Doris, a fine woman, died of a fever and left me with her three children and my two first. Man is not supposed to live alone, and a house must have a mistress and children a tender mother. Don't you agree, my lady?"

"Assuredly." Lady Willoughby was watching him curiously, and Stephanie surmised it was the lady's first social encounter with a merchant from the city.

"So, after a decent time, six months as I said and hard months they were to get through, I began to look around for a wife to comfort me and manage my household. I remembered my friend Tinkham and that he had a daughter. So, to cut it short, I went and called on Mrs Tinkham. She informed me her girl was visiting friends in the West End and there was no knowing when she would be home. Well, I'm not a patient man and not one to wait for weeks when my mind is settled. Mrs Tinkham assured me her daughter is quiet and well-behaved and obedient, which was all I needed to hear, knowing her family. So Mrs T. and I discussed the matter. Seventeen is thought young for marriage by some, but I say that will make it easier for her to learn my ways. In short, I made an offer and Mrs Tinkham and I have come to an agreement and Miss Hester Tinkham and I will be married in two weeks." He made the announcement with pride, his small eyes fastening on Hester. "Her mother says she will need no bride clothes because of all the blunt she put out for this visit. That pleases her and saves time. So," he ended with a beaming smile, "in three days I will send a coach for Miss Tinkham to carry her back to 29 Eldon Street. Quite a surprise, eh, Miss Tinkham? Your mother says you remember me most kindly and will be overcome with joy at the thought of a home of your own and not too distant from her."

"But that is not what I wish," faltered Hester.

He waved a fat hand. "It is what any girl wishes. It was my thought your mother should be the one to inform you of your good fortune, but she held you would be even more delighted if I brought the good news myself. She told me to remind you to thank Lady Willoughby for all her kindnesses to you."

"But, but," Hester stopped, then pulled herself together. "I am sensible of the honor, Mr Coburn, but I find I must refuse your offer."

"What?" Eyes and mouth rounded in surprise. "But you cannot, girl. Your mother and I have it settled. She is your guardian and if you have any fancy ideas in your head you can forget them. There are many who would jump with joy at my offer."

"Nevertheless, Mr Coburn, I will not marry you." Hester was even more firm than before.

"It is arranged and you will . . ." he began.

"But, Mr Coburn," Lady Willoughby intervened firmly, "I am surprised at your lack of sensibility. Any girl would be overcome by any offer delivered without warning and in such a peremptory fashion. Her mother should have thought of that, and I am surprised," she added loftily, "that she did not."

"We made our bargain and she said the girl would be as pleased as she was," he muttered.

"Her own view. No, Mr Coburn, even in the city such matters are not handled in this fashion, even though your own eagerness brought you here. You must return to Mrs Tinkham and tell her that her daughter refuses your offer."

"She'll be here and straighten that out, ma'am, in the switch of a cat's tail."

"You may tell her that if she wishes to discuss that, and other things, she may call on me Thursday afternoon, that is in two days, at three." She rose, gesturing to Stephanie to pull the bell rope, and waited as, scarlet and scowling, he levered himself up from the chair.

"I don't take this kindly," he growled. "And if Mrs T. has led me up the garden path I'll take that even less kindly. But," he drew himself up a little, "I will carry your message and I promise she'll come to call. And I'll be forgiving and not hold what the girl said against her." He lumbered over, snatched his hat from the footman, and stumped out.

Hester burst into tears, burying her face in her hands. "Oh, dear ma'am," she sobbed. "I am so ashamed. That my mother should send such a man to your house, who talked and behaved so . . . Forgive me."

"It is none of your doing," Lady Willoughby said briskly. "Cease weeping over something you could not help. Was that man truly a friend of your father's?"

Hester shook her head wildly. "No, ma'am, not a close friend, a business acquaintance only. He came to call twice, as I remember, briefly, but got along with my mother."

"So I perceive," Lady Willoughby said repressively. "And they have made a monetary agreement satisfactory to them both."

"But they cannot force me to marry him?" Hester stretched out one shaking hand. "That I could not bear."

"Of course not. It is outrageous. Don't go into the dismals thinking about it." Lady Willoughby's bracing tones brought the tears to a sniffle and a halt. "We must decide on our gowns for this evening, and that will make us forget that objectionable man."

But once in her room Hester began to cry again and Stephanie spent some time bathing her face and assuring her Cousin Doria would protect her, and if she did not recover she would give them all a miserable evening. That thought appealed to Hester's conscience and she cheered on the surface, but brooded through the following hours until she was reduced to a state of dumb despair.

By three o'clock Thursday the three were waiting in the small saloon. Hester, red-eyed, had three handkerchiefs in her reticule but her chin bravely tilted upward. Mrs Tinkham did not arrive.

"She is showing her independence and that she is not to be intimidated," Lady Willoughby nodded, her eyes bright. "Remember, Hester, to keep quiet unless you are asked a question. Do you both remember your manners." The knocker echoed below. "Ah, I am positively looking forward to this encounter."

Mrs Tinkham, in a plumed black hat and dark magenta dress and cloak, stalked past the footman announcing her and took a stance in the center of the room. The three rose and Lady Willoughby inclined her head and the girls gave a tiny dip.

"So kind of you to come, Mrs Tinkham." The voice was polite and neutral. "Pray take a chair."

The guest took the largest of the small armchairs and surveyed the three. "Good afternoon, ma'am, and," looking the girls over, "you two look well, I must say. Hester has quite improved in appearance. No wonder Mr Coburn came back all aglow for this to be settled." She tittered, but when there was no reply she stopped the sound and gazed angrily at Lady Willoughby. "I could not credit his tale, ma'am, that the chit had refused his flattering offer. He did say," she added grudgingly, "that it was her own doing with no prompting from you."

"There was no need to prompt her. It is obviously most inappropriate, and I am surprised, ma'am, that you lent yourself to it."

"How can you say that?" The black plumes trembled a bit. "It would be most advantageous for all. I cannot believe my little girl would be so ungrateful and disobedient. She has had time to think on it. Hester, you spoke hastily, did you not?"

Hester straightened, facing the imposing figure and holding her voice level. "No I did not, Mama. Mr

Coburn is repulsive to me and the situation he designs for me appalling. I will not mary him."

The face and figure seemed to puff out. "Hightytighty, miss. Who are you to say what you will do? Let me tell you if you've gotten any high-flying notions from staying here and mixing with the quality and are dragging your feathers to attract some lord who has taken your fancy, let me tell you you'll never trap such a one. No gentry is going to be caught by a skinny whey-faced daughter of a cit with no dowry. They're all laughing at your pretensions. Why, you couldn't even bring that green Sir Andrew up to scratch when you had the chance. So you'll take a sound man and be grateful to him all your life."

"How can you talk to Hester that way?" Stephanie, though she had sworn to keep silent, burst out hotly. "Hester is charming and has had successes with gentlemen."

"But not an offer among them," sneered her mother. She rounded on Stephanie. "And who are you, with your missy ways and highfalutin ideas, to take a stand for her? You've put ideas in her head and now she's going to get them out." She glared and Stephanie glared back.

"Mrs Tinkham, Stephanie, you forget yourselves," rebuked Lady Willoughby. "Mrs Tinkham, you should be ashamed to talk so to your daughter."

"And I'll not take that from you, lady though you are." The magenta bulk shifted around. "A mother speaks as she wishes to a stupid child. I have the ordering of the girl's life and I will take her home with me now. I'll see she makes a dutiful and obedient wife, you may be sure. Hester, go pack. Those gowns I've spent good money on won't be wasted now, even though they are above your station. Step lively, now."

"Mrs Tinkham, stop fulminating. You cannot make Hester go with you." It was a flat, stern statement.

The fleshy face reddened even more. "That I can, ma'am, and I'll thank you to keep out of this. I'll take her by force if need be. I am her guardian."

"But you are not." Lady Willoughby's fine eyes never moved from the face opposite.

Mrs Tinkham gasped, as if in horror, and one hand clutched at her chest. "How can you say so, ma'am? She is seventeen, and by her father's will she is subject to my commands."

Lady Willoughby sat back and gave a pitying smile. "I fear your memory is disordered, ma'am. Hester is four months over eighteen. Her birth date is recorded in the parish book and by her father. By his will she should have received both her independence of you and one half of his property, except for the house. Oh, do not protest. You have no leg to stand on. My own man of affairs went to consult with your husband's and learned the true facts."

"But I hold the will myself."

"No doubt, though you have obviously not consulted it in some time. But his own business man who saw to its drawing had a copy which, in such extraordinary circumstances and out of esteem for your husband, he allowed my man to peruse. Unless the money paid over the years from the business—it is apparently reposing in a bank under your name—is equally divided Hester will have to set proceedings under way to recover it."

The hat shook sideways. "Dear Hester would never do that to her mother."

"Yes I would," Hester burst out. "And gladly."

"Where could the child live? She has no home. Of course she will come to me and I will see she has her money and will not push the Coburn connection." Her hands were moving over her large reticule and the gaze she bent on Hester was obviously meant to be placatory.

"Hester has a home with me as long as she wishes," Lady Willoughby announced with composure. "I have long felt the need of a young companion. She is a dear girl and we deal very well together. She would be happy here."

"Oh, yes," Hester breathed, hands clasped, face ecstatic. "Oh, yes, dear ma'am."

"So that is settled. I shall send Mr Wainfield to call on Mr Tinkham's man and they can go to the bank together and see all is in order." She rose. "It was so wise of you to come, Mrs Tinkham, so all could be settled so satisfactorily."

Ponderously Mrs Tinkham rose also. "Not to me, my lady, but I can do nothing to overset your iniquitous actions."

"Come now," Lady Willoughby spoke with a benign condescension, "it is not me you would be fighting but your husband's expressed desires, and the law. You could not win, you know. I will cherish Hester as if she were my own. You will be relieved to have her care removed from your shoulders and happy she has a pleasant home. Good day."

Reluctantly Mrs Tinkham moved to the door. She turned, shot a fierce glare at Hester, cried out, "Viper. Never darken my door," and stalked into the hall.

Hester ran to Lady Willoughby. "Oh, dear ma'am, how can I thank you? You did mean it? Now I will never have to fear again."

Lady Willoughby leaned down and kissed her cheek. "Were you really afraid she would take you away? Poor child. I do indeed mean it. You will be a most pleasant companion."

"Where do I stand?" Stephanie asked a little plaintively. "May I not be a companion also?"

"Of course, dear child. But you are in quite a different case for you do have your home in Dorset. But of course you will stay with me as long as you wish. That was our understanding." She trilled a little laugh. "It is a long time since I have had the pleasure of confounding a fraud and I enjoyed it thoroughly."

Chapter 10

LADY Willoughby was reading her mail during nuncheon, a few days after the routing of Mrs Tinkham, and gave a light shriek. "Lady Diana Inverskaid is giving a rout! Next Wednesday. We are bid to come at seven. So early! She has not entertained in years."

"What sort of rout would it be?" Stephanie could envision nothing of that description surrounding Lady Diana.

"There is no imagining. But at the bottom is written by hand, quite prettily, a secretary no doubt, 'Do not wear your best gowns.' Imagine that!"

"Perhaps there will be games," offered Hester.

"A possibility. Mother often told me that people

were devoted to games of all kinds thirty years ago, particularly at house parties. But Lady Diana . . . today . . ." She shook her head and the white lace cap slipped a little. "I will accept instantly."

"Good," said Lord Airde from the doorway. "I stopped to make sure the invitation had arrived." From his clothes, he had been riding, and the plain white stock somehow emphasized the bones and hollows of his face.

"You know about this?" Cousin Doria demanded.

"Not a thing, my dear, except that Aunt Di summoned me last evening, took me from cards, too." Amusement made his expression lively. "My great-aunt allowed me five minutes to hear she was bored, that society today is stiff and dull—though how she perceives that since she never goes out I cannot tell you—and needed some stirring up and she was going to do it. She did add the affair would be small, only eighty or so, and none would be ancient. I approved and was dismissed."

Lady Willoughby shook her head again and the cap slipped further. "Why are we told not to wear our best?"

"What?" He strode across the room, plucked the note from her hand and laughed out loud. "No one could guess. I advise an elegant simplicity that you can move in easily for the lady has an antic wit. Dear Doria, you should always wear your headgear at an angle, takes off ten years. Ladies, your devoted servant," and he bowed out.

"Well!" Hands went to her head. "Is it true that a

cap at a slant is becoming? I'll try it. Airde has such a
good eye. What shall we wear?"

A stately procession of coaches was debouching into
Chandos Street, advancing slowly without the customary confusion, and departing. The three mounted a
wide staircase to the first floor and to the second which
was brightly lighted as were the rooms on either side.
As they left their cloaks with maids Stephanie felt they
had achieved the elegant simplicity advised by Airde
for her green and Hester's blue were of silk that fell
in · soft folds beneath embroidered overskirts that
matched the small ruffles at neck and hem. She rather
wished they had not been so restrained as she watched
the elaborate gowns of satin and taffeta, the nodding
feathers and elaborate jewelry, as a procession moved
toward the ballroom, even though they could in no
way have rivaled the others. Many of the people seemed
acquainted and greetings were acknowledged in stately
and reserved fashion.

"All the oldest and stiffest families," whispered
Cousin Doria. "Some so high in the instep they won't
go to Almack's. And not one of them is tottering."

The ballroom was dazzling. Not only were the three
huge chandeliers as bright as the sun, but sconces,
backed by mirrors and between long mirrors, were so
filled with light the candles could not be counted. The
line of guests was moving at a smart pace down · the
left hand side of the room, crossing in front of the
towering mantelpiece a-blaze with light and color, and
then lining the right wall. Hiding the useful portion of

the fireplace was a low gold platform surrounded by what appeared to be a small house.

"*Is* that a house?" Stephanie breathed in awe.

"Not a house but a howdah," Airde chuckled softly behind her. "Knew she had one but I've never seen it. For elephant hunting, you know."

Hester missed a step and recovered. "Hunting?" she asked faintly.

"Not in here, or of a different kind, Miss Tinkham," he reassured her. "Really used only in India."

Then they were bowing before it. The frame was of elaborately carved and gilded wood and it was lined with pink silk drawn at the top to resemble a tent. At the front, above a gilded balustrade which completed the gold frame, Lady Diana sat, bolt upright, smiling at her guests and inclining her head as each passed. The platform and the howdah raised her so she was a good two feet above the highest of the plumes. Her eyes sparkled as vividly as her tiara and wide necklace and she was looking very pleased with herself.

As the three curtseyed, and Airde and Seddon bowed beside them, she held up her hand. A footman with white wand stepped forward and halted the procession.

"How do you like my howdah, Esham?" Though her voice was quiet it had a clear carrying quality anyone would be proud to possess.

"Not so magnificent as its occupant," he bowed again, "but magnificent."

"Well spoken, as always." In anyone else the sound accompanying it might have been a giggle. "This should stir up all the antiquated sticklers, and high time. Remain after the others go, all of you, for I wish to speak to you." Her gaze swept over them and she nodded, the white wand was raised and they passed to the right. All the guests were remaining in line, peering surreptitiously around the room and conversing in whispers.

When no more were seen coming through the doors two tall men in pink tunics, loose trousers and turbans stepped to the right of the howdah, produced two long golden horns, and blew a loud but musical blast. Everyone jumped and Lady Di looked pleased. Into the following silence stepped Blodgett, an imposing figure in butler's black and white.

"Ladies and gentlemen," he began, and his voice carried the length of the room clearly but without shouting. "You will now enjoy a variety of activities. Each new one will be signaled by the trumpets. I will then direct you. At the end of each event the trumpets will sound again." There was a rustling and murmuring around the walls. "You will now each of you be offered a basket containing numbers on cards, ladies white, gentlemen red. You will each pick a card as the basket is offered and hold it."

Two lines of footmen, also in pink and gold, came swiftly through the doors and marched down the two lines holding out gilt baskets to each guest. It all moved so swiftly none dared linger over the choice but plunged a hand in and jerked out a card. Stephanie's was number 37. As the footmen disappeared amid rising voices the trumpets sounded.

"We will begin with a promenade," Blodgett instructed. "Each gentleman will match the number on his card with that of a lady and then form in line. You

will all hold your cards at shoulder level. You have
five minutes to find your partner." He pulled out a
watch. "Those who have not found the proper number
will retire to the end of the room."

The gasp was nearly as loud as the trumpets, but
there was only a slight hesitation before some of the
men began to push forward, cards held up, peering at
ladies as ladies peered at gentlemen. Lines broke,
people began hurrying, giving little cries of pleasure
or surprise. Stephanie's opposite number was a thin,
military-looking man in red velvet with grey hair and
sharp eyes. They had just found each other and were
laughing when the trumpets silenced them. A little
group in the center was still unpaired.

"Kindly move to the sofas in the rear," Blodgett directed, and they almost slunk away amid cries of
"Shame Shame." A hidden orchestra began to play
what was obviously a march and in two minutes the
double line was parading around the hall, watched by
Lady Di, but ignoring her as they introduced themselves and exclaimed.

"Chap must have been a sergeant-major," Stephanie's partner, who allowed he was an earl and a retired general, nodded toward Blodgett. "But he's been
trained well to be more than that. Wish I'd had him
in my outfit. Now, Langley, you must be . . ." and
she found she was talking and laughing with him with
complete ease.

They were only allowed ten minutes and no time to
fall into silences when the trumpets blew and the room
halted obediently. Faces turned with curiosity toward
Blodgett.

"Though many of you already know each other it is
our intention that you meet others. You have just done
so. You are enjoined to speak warmly to each other
every time you encounter each other during the rest of
the evening. If you do not you will be expelled from
the following event. We will proceed." There was positively a benign note in Blodgett's voice. "The gentlemen will kindly move to the center, the ladies remaining on an outer circle. At the trumpet the ladies will
proceed to choose a partner for a short waltz but he
must not be related to you nor your escort." There
came little shrieks of horror and the men of all ages
began to look self-conscious. Stephanie tried to locate
Airde, since he had not brought them. "The gentlemen
will stand separately," Blodgett continued. "The ladies
have five minutes. All without partners then will retire."

The shrieks were louder and protests of "No" arose,
but only a few. There came the blast. Some ladies
moved forward uncertainly, others, many of them
older, pushed ahead, laughing and determined. There
was confusion and swirling of gowns and even a cry
of "I was here first" and a proud "I can't dance with
two" and again came the trumpets. Thanks to her foresight, Stephanie had found Airde quickly, though she
was conscious of a blonde bearing toward him with a
hunting look and saw Hester out-distanced to Sir Andrew by a swift brunette. Came the trumpets, more
scurrying, and a waltz from the orchestra.

Airde was laughing as he put his arm around her.
"Aunt Di is stirring them up all right. And enjoying
the process herself, she isn't even trying to hide her

grin. You can feel every one beginning to loosen up."

"Where does she get the ideas?" Stephanie leaned back to look up into the laughing eyes.

"They had all kinds of notions in her days, made a point of thinking up different ploys to make a party lively. This is pretty staid by comparison with what I've heard. And she's keeping it all short and fast, which is wise."

They had only circled the floor twice when they were halted again. Stephanie could feel a lightening such as she had never felt at a ball. The normally composed faces were relaxed and merry, dresses not quite so tightly adjusted to figures, a few neckcloths loosened. If this was how routs and balls were run forty years ago it was a pity they had ever changed.

"It is now the gentlemen's turn to go hunting," Blodgett was calling. "Ladies to the center, standing separately. Gentlemen you are on your honor to choose a lady to whom you have never been introduced. We realize you will have difficulty with so many beauties to choose from, but, gentlemen, you have just five minutes and the race is to the swift."

With side glances and some falsetto laughter and disclaimers the ladies moved to the center, and Stephanie wished she could move as self-confidently as some of the real beauties. She did hope she would not have to retreat to the sofas because no one had wanted her for a partner.

But the trumpet echoes had hardly died when her hand was lifted and a red-haired young man was laughing. "Almost made a race of it, saw two others heading for you. I so hoped this would happen, that I'd have a chance . . . I've had my eye on you all evening. My name's Rainford and I know you're Miss Langley, asked the man you promenaded with, he wished me luck, too. Here's the music. Can't miss a minute of it."

He whirled her off at top speed and kept her talking and listening so gayly that she never had time to look for her friends. He came from Scotland, was on leave from the navy, asked if he could call and her direction, and launched into a tale of a leave in St. Petersburg. She was laughing helplessly when the dance ended and begged him to come soon and tell her what happened when he got lost in the embassy. He vowed he would and they parted with bright regret at the trumpets.

Cousin Doria was rejoicing. "What a most *satisfactory* affair," she gasped. "Look, Lady Di is laughing too. What next?"

"You are now to embark on a treasure hunt," Blodgett told them after the trumpets had brought attentive quiet. "On this floor and on the one above are hidden ten small gold dishes decorated with diamonds. Only the ten rooms with open doors may be searched. Nothing is to be opened, they are in sight, not within anything. They are engraved with a J on the bottom for they come from Jaipur for they were a gift. There can be no substitutions." There was a flood of laughter at the idea and he paused. "The finders will return to this room, with their trophies, which are to be kept as mementos." People began to move apart, edge toward the doors though watching Blodgett for any new surprise. "One half hour is allowed for the search. When summoned as before you will return here." The trumpets then freed them and there was an undignified rush; the pink curtains of the howdah were being drawn.

Filled with an impish determination to find a gold dish, Stephanie whirled around, waved at Airde who was starting forward, and dodged around two large dowagers who were trotting eagerly, one saying "The bedrooms are sure to have some" and the other "Mary Aston is so *nosey* she'll surely find one," and sped toward the stairs. On the way she encountered the earl-general who waved and called "good luck." The second of the two floors would not be searched so quickly as this one, she was sure. At the top of the stairs she looked down at the milling, colorful crowd that was unashamedly pushing its way toward open doors on either side of the hall.

There were six open doors in the hall above. She hurried to the first which showed a large bedroom elaborately furnished in blue, two sets of corner shelves crowded with bibelots, a well-furnished dressing table, a book case. She walked around hastily but nothing gold caught her eye. The other rooms were equally crowded with small boxes of vermeil or chased gold and silver, scent bottles, fans, porcelain, it would take a long time to go through such. The last room on the right was a study, austere, a mounted stag's head, two mounted trout, books, and a case of Indian statuettes in gold and silver whose postures were so embarrassing she looked away. But there *must* be one in here . . . A gold dish would have looked jaunty on the point of a stag's horn, but too obvious. She looked among the collection of knives on the top of a low bookcase, the tops of the books, to the rods that held dark red

draperies at the window. At the far corner she caught
a glint of gold. Running to the nearest chair, a massive
piece, she tugged and shoved it to the window and
climbed on the seat but could not reach the rod. A surge
of voices and cries came from the hall. She clambered
down, ran to the black fireplace, seized the poker and
got back on the chair, thankful her skirt was full. She
raised the poker, pushed at the shining gold and it came
forward a little. Yes, it was a dish. She leaned sideways
placing the tip of the poker behind the dish and pushed
again. A glowing sparkling object began to fall toward
her. Dropping the poker she reached up with both
hands, caught the cup and felt herself begin to sway.

Hands caught her around the waist, steadied her,
and lifted her down. A bright-eyed sandy-haired young
man was laughing down at her. "I should have come
five minutes earlier. I saw the thing from the doorway
and started for it. Then I saw you. I could have pushed
you out of the way, ma'am, and jumped for it. Please
remember I suppressed my baser instincts."

"Oh, I promise. A true gentleman you are, sir, and
I am grateful it was one such who saw me teetering.
You could even have snatched it before it reached my
hands."

"Some would have," he said gaily. "My reward for
my restraint will be, I hope, your friendship. May I
escort you down? My name is Warebrook."

Clutching her dish Stephanie managed a dip and
murmured her name and walked with him to the door.
From the room across the hall came an affronted cry:
"You beast! I saw it first. You watched my eyes!"

"But you weren't nippy enough, dear Lady Sophy," rumbled a contented voice. "I got it."

"A gentleman wouldn't have snatched it ahead of a lady!"

"There are no gentlemen where gold is concerned, as you well know," and there came a bellow of laughter and another cry of "You beast!"

"How fortunate I was," Stephanie gurgled. "I do thank you again for your forbearance."

"Come along." He took her elbow and they ran for the stairs, pushing through the crowd that still milled through the hall. "I'll be cheering for you."

They found the ballroom filled with gold wicker chairs and tables bearing pink and white cloths and footmen carrying trays of champagne goblets which were being seized and emptied between murmurs of "hot work that." The successful hunters were being lined before the howdah. Warebrook, still holding her elbow, marched her forward. "Have dinner with me," he begged as they halted and at her nod, "I'll hold that table there and get friends."

As the trumpet blew and the nine were looking at each other with satisfaction a dowager in purple taffeta sailed down the center aisle, two black plumes hanging from the back of her head, gown caught up on one side nearly to her knee, but holding above her head in triumph the tenth dish. There was such a glow on her narrow face that cheers broke out and she took her place with a flirt of her skirt and a toss of the dangling feathers.

From the howdah Lady Di nodded delightedly. "You have all done well, though that I expected. May you enjoy your trophies. Blodgett, call the names of the winners." There were cheers and calls as each stepped forward. Stephanie was the youngest, and heard a loud "Bravo" to the side as she dipped.

"You will now have a collation," Blodgett informed them. "It will be followed by an entertainment."

There was a scurrying for tables, voices calling, as they settled. The curtains of the howdah were drawn again. Stephanie was making her way to the table where Warebrook was standing when Airde intercepted her. "Well done, Miss Langley. I am proud of you. I have a table here."

"But I am engaged for another table, thank you." She smiled sweetly, finding it very satisfactory to show Airde he was not the only gentleman to desire her company.

The collation was delicious but light and with only champagne served there was no possibility the company could become comatose. The laughter and voices mounted in volume and gaiety until it sounded as if everyone was talking at once. Warebrook and his two friends, a serious young man and a shy ash-blonde, were pleasant companions. Stephanie glanced around once for Airde but could not find where he was seated. When the last course was completed the tables were whisked away and they were left in their chairs.

The trumpets appeared again and Blodgett took charge. "You will rise and retreat with your table companions to the walls. There the ladies will turn to the right, gentlemen to the left and you will commence walking, greeting every third person you pass. This is to enable the chairs to be placed in rows and will not last long. You may then break rows and find places. Miss Ogilvy and Mr McKown will lead you in song."

Obediently all rose, retreated, turned, marched and greeted with rising enthusiasm which was cut off before it became noisy, though there was a certain confusion over the seating. During that Lord Rainford seized Stephanie, muttering "timed it just right" and had them in place as the trumpets sounded above a final scuttling. A young woman and a young man, both handsome and in Highland costume, appeared in one corner at the left of the howdah and began a rousing *John Peel*. By the time the chorus was reached some of the audience were joining in and all were singing by the second verse. They kept on singing, without pause, guided from song to ballad, which they had known in their youth, nigh forgotten, and now recalled energetically. And abruptly it stopped.

There was a last flourish of trumpets. "You will now leave," Blodgett told them. "Lady Diana says it is not necessary to take your farewells of her for she could see that you have enjoyed yourselves."

"To the nines," shouted a deep voice. "Thank you, Di." "Hooray for Lady Di," came from another quarter followed by other calls as, still obedient, all headed for the doors.

Stephanie remembered she had been told to remain and reluctantly had to refuse Lord Rainford's request to escort her home and gladly granted him permission to call. It was at the end of his somewhat lingering farewell that a sardonic Airde appeared and removed her over Rainford's protests, and marched her to the howdah.

Lady Di did not look the least tired but alert and mischievous as she surveyed the five. "It was a good party," she told them proudly. "They won't forget it. Stirred them up, took them back to when affairs were amusing. Those who weren't asked will be furious," she added happily.

"Aunt Di," Airde moved closer to the howdah, "it was a bloody wonderful party and you know it. Don't know how you got it all together. I always heard you should have been running the empire and not just India. But may I humbly ask why?"

"I've been bored a long time," she told him simply. "Couldn't think how to entertain myself. Then appeared the Langley girl, thanks to you. She has no fortune and no high position. Nick Langley and I were—great friends." For a moment the large black eyes looked into Stephanie's. "Decided to do something for his granddaughter. "Now," and her voice became complacent, "she's launched at the top because she was here. She's met top people, saw she captured two sound men, and she can marry anyone she chooses. She won't have to hang around waiting for you, Esham, to make up your mind." She laughed. "If you could see your face, my dear. Good for you to have some plain speaking. Go along, now, all of you. No, I'm not tired, but I knew I had to keep it short for them. No stamina today." She sniffed. "I'll take your thanks as said." She clapped her hands and pulled the pink silk curtain across the front of the howdah. Footmen were materializing as they walked down the room to the stairs. Stephanie, clutching her gold dish, stole a glance at Airde, but his expression was impenetrable.

Lady Diana's predictions came true in part in some of the invitations that flowed to Montague Street. Cousin Doria and Stephanie attended two very formal dinners where it was hard to believe they had seen their hosts and the guests excitedly searching from room to room. There was an exclusive violin concert and, it seemed, more balls. Stephanie encountered an inscrutable Airde and took to treating him with a certain aloofness, to show she had not paid attention to Lady Diana's words, and she could but regret he did not seem to notice. Her new friends, Lord Warebrook and Lord Rainford, became pleasingly attentive and enlivened her days and evenings, for both set themselves to please her and enjoyed their rivalry as much as she did. She was truly sorry when Lord Rainford, complaining bitterly, had to return to his ship. Suddenly Airde appeared more frequently and alternately delighted and exasperated her. Even Lord Maleby devoted a little time to her. But she and Hester missed Sir Andrew. His social life had become the care of Lady Donnington, who had not been at the rout, and he confessed when he came to tea that between the lady and Lord Maleby his time was over-crowded.

"He does not need us any more," Hester mourned.

"We are his first friends and he is not one to forget that," Stephanie said with assurance. "He may need us again." And she hoped he would, along with the ambiguous Lord Airde.

Chapter 11

LORD Airde sat at a side desk in the outer office of Lord Fanningthorpe on Downing Street. He was reading a batch of reports from India, wondering why he had to bother with such a distant place, and waiting for his chief to return from a conference. He wondered if the dispatches from the Peninsula had arrived.

It was evident they had not, for his Lordship, frowning, strode in. "No word yet, Airde. Don't know what's wrong with men and horses these days. Messenger should have been here by noon. We've got to know what Wellington's planning and what he needs before we can approve, don't we? Now we'll have to wait—everyone's going out of town, one reason or another." He stalked into his office, looked at the desk and stalked out. "I'm off. You'd better stay another hour, just in case some spavined horse does get here from Plymouth or Portsmouth or Newhaven or wherever some frightened captain puts in his ship. If anything comes bring it to me wherever I am, butler will know, this evening. After that, keep it here." He nodded and left. Airde resignedly turned back to a long letter about the problems presented by the maharajah of Jaipur.

The hour was nearly gone when a dusty, weary messenger entered, explaining his horse had broken a leg, and handed over a small sealed package. Airde signed for it and reflected a dispatch rider's life was hard and wondered what the wily Wellington had planned and how much he would reveal to their Lordships. He picked up the packet and started toward the inner office when he was halted by the hearty voice of Lord Maleby.

"Ah, Airde, glad to see you." He moved into the room.

"Good afternoon, sir." Airde was sure Maleby had noted the packet in his hand and the three seals.

"His Lordship in?" Maleby asked genially. "There is a memorandum he promised me today, something about a West Indies merchantman, just captured, some diplomat on board."

"His Lordship has left for the day," Airde told him. "He said nothing about a memorandum for you."

"He has a wise view of what is due a hard-working gentleman at the end of the afternoon," Maleby approved even more genially. "It's not immediately important, dispute between departments as to who gets her, but we might see if he left it on his desk."

Airde was reluctant but Maleby was moving toward the inner office and he could do nothing but follow. The man had the effrontery of an ox, probably that was what amused the Prince Regent. Maleby advanced to the desk.

"There is no paper here," Airde pointed out.

"Wouldn't expect it to be out by itself," Maleby reproved him. "But those two piles of papers, now. You're in his confidence. Just glance through them. Name of the ship is *Lady Anne,* would be on the heading, or something."

Reluctantly, and as swiftly as possible, Airde riffled through the two heaps of papers, minor memoranda, letters begging for favors, nothing of any importance. He straightened them. "There is no memorandum about a ship, sir."

"He probably overlooked it, in the press of other business. I'll send Seddon for it in a day or so." Lord Maleby walked toward the door. "That reminds me. I've been seeing you with that charming daughter of my old friend General Langley. You must bring her down for a weekend. Bring her friend and Seddon too, I'll tell him he is coming. I'd like your opinion on some horses. Place is in Sussex, a comfortable day's drive, near Bexhill. Yes, by Jove." He stopped and faced Airde. "What's today? Wednesday? Bring them down on Friday."

"You are too kind, sir." Airde made a little bow. "May I consult Miss Langley and send you word?"

"Of course, but tell her I won't take a no." Lord Maleby clapped him on the shoulder. "See you Friday," he nodded and left.

Now what is that all about, Airde wondered as he hurried back to the inner office. He must take the packet and start after Lord Fanningthorpe. But the packet was not on the desk, nor on the two heaps of papers. Incredulous, he ran his hands through his hair. He had had it in his hand when Maleby came in, was still holding it when he came here. He had put it down so he could go quickly through those confounded piles. Then he had walked back with Maleby. He dropped to one knee to peer under desk and chairs. Nothing. So Maleby had taken it. He would recognize it, knew what was awaited, and that it was of great importance.

Airde sighed and straightened. It was his responsibility. He must get it back, and quickly. The first place to try to catch him was his office, the second his house. It seemed a long way to the Admiralty and took too long to locate Maleby's office. The outer one held only Seddon, bent over a large ledger.

"No. Lord Maleby's not here," Seddon answered Airde's quiet query. "He put his head in the door, told Meriney to come with him and me to finish this, and they went off. I say, Airde, an aide is not supposed to be a clerk, is he?"

In spite of his impatience Airde paused to look at the disconsolate face. "No. Your wound all healed?"

"Yes, sir. Not a twinge."

"Why don't you put in for a return to your regiment? It need not go through Maleby. I'll help you. Where did he go?"

"He sent for his coach to come to the side door. He said to Meriney they were going to his house."

"My thanks. We'll see about that request." He smiled reassuringly and started for a hackney. He'd reach Maleby's place faster by horseback than by phaeton because the streets were so clogged.

It was an hour before he reached home and could turn his horse's head to the northwest. And in spite of using side streets and alleys for shortcuts it was nearly another before he dismounted at the pretentious mansion. A rugged butler opened the door.

"Lord Maleby," Airde told him brusquely. "Lord Airde is calling. Send someone to walk my mount."

"Lord Maleby said he was not to be disturbed," the butler intoned.

"He will be by me." Airde stepped through the doorway and gestured to a footman. "You. Go walk my horse. You," he swung on the butler, "go and inform Lord Maleby I am here." He saw a lighted door at one side. "I will wait in there." Without a backward glance he walked into the small attending room. As he went through the doorway he saw the butler mounting the stairs and a footman appearing with more candles. Twice he paced around the room then, since he would obviously be kept waiting, chose a chair.

It was twenty-seven minutes before Maleby, in evening dress, sauntered through the doorway. "My dear Airde. Of course I've been expecting you ever since I discovered I had picked up by chance a packet from your office that is definitely not mine. I thought first I would send it around. But then I realized your devotion to duty would bring you here in person, as it did, more quickly than I anticipated. Forgive me for keeping you waiting but I was preparing for the evening and my valet would not let me go until I was completed to his satisfaction. I knew you would understand."

"Certainly, sir." Airde rose and nodded. "I, in turn, was sure you would send it to me but rather than put you, or one of your people, to inconvenience I came myself."

"Very thoughtful," Maleby now had a purring note. "I have come to deliver it to you in person."

He held out his right hand, with the packet, front cover up, and dropped it in Airde's outstretched hand. His eyes on Maleby's face, one of Airde's fingers moved across the nearest seal, and Maleby's eyes flickered. The seal was warm to the touch. So were the other two he could feel as he put the packet in his pocket. "I am sorry to have given you any trouble, sir," he said gently.

"It was nothing," Maleby returned as gently. "I gather it is not of importance or you would not be so —unobserving with government dispatches." He was watching the other man closely.

"I assure you I regret my lack of observation," Airde returned easily.

Maleby walked across the room, the dark evening coat and light breeches emphasizing his height and heavy shoulders. In a wall mirror Airde looked slender beside him.

"We'll say no more about it. It will be our joint secret. I would not wish for any blemish to appear on your distinguished record." Maleby's voice was almost caressing and Airde bowed, very slightly. "And I will have the pleasure of welcoming you and your friends Friday at Hawksdown. It is just above Bexhill, as I said. Not so fine a place as another I possess, but agreeable. We will all have an opportunity to become better acquainted." He nodded. Airde bent his head and left the room.

"We must all go," Airde told Stephanie when he found her in the small library after an early dinner. "He insisted, twice. It is a hope that it may mean that Seddon has advanced in his favor, which might make his life easier. You and Miss Tinkham can be ready by Friday morning?"

"Of course." The question was surprising. "We will be happy to go on the chance the party may be of benefit to Sir Andrew. Will Cousin Doria approve?"

"I am sure she will. How agreeable that you can be ready so quickly. I have known ladies to demand a week's notice. We will take my traveling coach for since there are two of you no abigail will be needed and there will surely be a maid for ladies. I'll mount Seddon. It will take most of the day. We will return on Monday."

"But why this sudden invitation?" she asked. She had more questions but started with the obvious.

He stretched out his long legs and regarded her seriously for a moment. His dark hair was ruffled and his cheeks seemed more hollow than usual, his hazel eyes brighter. Why, he's almost handsome, she thought with surprise. He's different, not so beautiful as Sir Andrew, of course, but interesting and the word effective came to her mind. She became aware he had been studying her face as she had been his and blushed and dropped her eyes.

"Yes," he said, as if in answer to some inner thought, then, "I am not completely sure of the reason. But you and Hester are to have nothing to do but enjoy yourselves, you understand? Now, pray ask your Cousin Doria to spare me a few minutes."

"She is readying herself for an evening of whist at Mrs Colton's and deciding whether to wear her fourth best necklace or her sixth best so as to look poor and guileless. There, the coach must be here, for she is coming down."

Looking brightly pleased in gray and only a turquoise necklace she met them in the hall. Stephanie went back to the library for her book and emerged as the front door opened. Hurrying to join them, she wished Cousin Doria the confounding of all opponents and walked down the short steps to the pavement and watched Airde hand the lady into her coach.

It was the time between day and night when the twilight turns blue and street lamps are not yet lit and the golden gleam of candles at windows vies with the remnants of the day. It was very quiet, and the air smelled of cut grass and fresh earth. Suddenly Stephanie was homesick for the country. As Airde returned to her she seized his arm. "It is so lovely and peaceful. Let us walk for a few minutes, my lord. We might almost be in the country. I allow I get homesick on occasion for fields and trees. It would be only ten minutes to Montague Square and back. There are some trees there."

He looked down at the eager, pleading face upturned to his. "It's not proper, you without cloak or bonnet or abigail." A smile began at the corners of his mouth.

"Come." She gave a tug. "We don't have to be proper all the time. That is so dull. You know it would be pleasant."

"It would be. I succumb against my better judgment, as seems to be my habit when you are so enticing. Wait here. I will tell the footman to stay by the door and to tell no one."

On his return she tucked her hand inside his arm and they strolled to the corner and across Crawford Street to the long narrow square. It was still quiet except for some birds and a little rustle in the trees and a horse clopping in the distance.

"How companionable it is to walk with you!" Stephanie exclaimed with wonder. "I had not thought of that."

"We've been companionable under other circumstances," he pointed out gently.

"True. And I should have known you would be, for, underneath, I am convinced our tastes are much alike." She gave him a mischievous glance. "I'll never forget your face when you saw us as maids."

They joined in laughter. "I was in a quake all the time for fear we could not get out of that stew but it was so hilarious I could scarce keep my mind on my duty."

For a flash she wondered if kissing her had been a duty and wished she could ask but that would be too provocative. "It is most helpful to know to whom I can turn for company when I weary of being proper," she substituted and hoped he read no double meanings into the words. "Why, we have circled the square. It has seemed such a short walk."

"It has indeed, but I am taking you home before you demand to walk on to Portman Square or to the park. Any minute now there will be people and carriages in the streets and you would be noticed."

"You are right," she sighed. "But confess you were glad of the stroll on such a pretty evening."

"I have enjoyed it." His voice was warm. "Yes, I would be happy to stroll with you again as we just have."

They crossed Crawford Street. From the shadows at the corner a figure jumped at them. Stephanie gave a shriek. In one movement Airde had thrust her behind him, raised his cane, knocked aside the descending stick, landed a hard blow on the arm that held it and thrust toward the face. Another figure had circled behind them. As the first man retreated a cudgel came down on Airde's head and he crumpled slowly. Stephanie shrieked again. The figures ran down Crawford Street. She knelt on the pavement. Airde's eyes were closed. For a moment her heart failed her; she could not bear to have anything happen to this man. She must get help, get him to the house. She scrambled to her feet. But if she left him those men might return. She could at least scream again if she saw them. She must find someone to go for help.

The door of the corner house opened and two figures came out, hats, canes, knee breeches, they must be gentlemen. She called "Help. Do come here."

The two men paused on the pavement. "Did you hear something, Spence?" asked one.

"Perhaps," the other agreed cautiously.

"Sounded like 'help'."

"It did, now you mention it, Gatney."

Stephanie hurried a few paces. "Oh, kind sirs, do come."

One turned to the other and nodded. "Heard it again."

"So did I. A lady. There." He pointed with his cane.

"Can't be a lady, old man. No hat, no cloak, no abigail. You're above yourself already."

"Not foxed. Look again. Lady. Sounds like one, too."

"Still say she can't be one. What does she want?"

"Don't know. Have to be careful."

"You're right—might be a trap."

"Oh, stop arguing." Stephanie looked back at Airde and took two more steps and raised her voice. "I need you."

"For what?" asked one brightly.

"To go four houses down and tell the footman to come with the second man to this corner. And quick."

"Why?" asked the second one.

"She wants us to go to a strange house for a footman, Gatney."

"Do we know the people?"

"Oh." In fury Stephanie's voice rose again. "You— dolts. Go and get the men. My escort has been attacked." She had remembered in time not to use Airde's name.

"Gentleman?"

"Yes. Yes."

"Then no matter what we must go for the footman. If her escort's a gentleman she *must* be a lady, on this street, Gatney. Your servant, ma'am." He swept off his hat.

"And hurry," she cried after them, and ran back to Airde.

From beside him she watched the two young men go up the steps, knock, point and descend. As they turned away they both raised their hats in her direction.

By the time the footmen arrived Airde was moving and trying to sit up. One on either side, they helped him to the house and into the attending room, Stephanie following with hat and cane. They brought a basin of water so she could bathe his face and the bruise on the back of his head. Though the skin was broken it did not appear deep or serious. He stirred when she finished and gave her a wry smile.

"Not a very heroic figure, your escort, Stephanie."

"Oh, you were." She was sitting on the floor, washing the dirt from his hands. "You were so fast. You'd have knocked the man out if it had not been for the second."

"Too true. I should have turned more quickly."

"You couldn't have. Oh, Airde," she dried one hand. "If only I had not wished to go for a walk this would not have happened." She could not hold back a tiny sob. "I am distressed beyond measure."

"Pray don't be, my dear. It might have happened, anywhere. Without you beside me I'd have been in a bucket. There's nothing much wrong, I'm sure." He looked at the hat on the sofa beside him. "See, the hat got the worst of it." He pulled himself straig__ __nd held out a hand to help her rise. "Carry your kindness a little further and order a brandy for me and ask one of the men to get me a hackney."

She watched anxiously while he downed the brandy and some color came back in his face. "Should you go alone?"

"Certainly. Pray accept my deepest gratitude for everything. I can say again it was a delightful stroll." He smiled and left, a footman on either side but walking quite steadily.

How odd it had been, she thought when in her room. The two men rushing out at Airde. He had been so skillful, experienced, against the first attacker. If it had not been for the man coming behind him . . . How fortunate the hat had been so sturdy. They would laugh about that some day. But there was that dreadful moment when he had crumpled and lain as if dead . . . She put her hands to her face. She had felt such a strong emotion, had cried to herself she could not bear to have anything happen to him. She took down her hands and looked at the black window. It was true that if he were not in her life it would be quite dull. But one might feel that way about any good friend. Of course she must never let him know she so valued his friendship for she was not one to hang on any man's sleeve nor he one to allow it. Of course they would continue to be friends. But, she went back to her first thought, why had it happened? A common footpad did not seem the answer. It would not be too forward to ask a question.

Chapter 12

SHE had no opportunity to ask for the next time she saw him was when he arrived with Sir Andrew and the traveling coach on Friday morning.

"You will be traveling in style and comfort, my loves, which do not always go together, for Esham's coach is not only well padded but well sprung." Cousin Doria pointed out the window as the two gentlemen dismounted from their horses and two footmen carried out four boxes. "You can but enjoy the drive and the visit, even though it is rather far for comfort." She hastened to welcome the men, offered port and biscuits to sustain them, refrained from reproach when they refused, and waved to coach and horsemen as they trotted down the street.

Stephanie regretted that from the back seat they could not see straight ahead, but the windows in the doors were large enough to give them quite good views. Once across the river, which, they vowed, they must be brought to see again, they were soon watching little hills and trees and fields. Then the coach stopped and Airde came into the carriage to sit facing them, and agreed the Thames was worth any number of visits from the shore and even by barge.

"We are taking the Eastbourne road," he went on, "for it is faster than by way of Tunbridge Wells though not so picturesque."

"Will we see castles and great houses?" Hester asked breathlessly. "I never have."

"Not many, for they hide themselves, but we'll try," and pointed out a distant roof that could be glimpsed over trees. He left them shortly and Seddon took his place. He was not informative, for he had never been in Kent or Sussex, but shared their pleasure at the sight of thatched cottages, hedged fields and villages. They lunched at East Grinstead, a name Stephanie deplored as not being appealing. With fresh horses they headed south through a forest, part of the ancient Weald, and then over field-covered hills that rolled over and over and Airde said they were the downs. Once they turned aside to view from a distance a reddish-pink, square, turreted castle surrounded by a moat, which was Hurstmonceaux, a name Stephanie could approve.

Winding, tree-walled lanes dipped and rose and

came at last to pillars and a drive that mounted to a low plateau of lawns and the house called Hawksdown. Lord Maleby met them at the front door in the forecourt which was enclosed by two wings as high as the center portion. As Stephanie descended she saw his gaze go over in appraisal the coach and horses before he spread his hands in welcome.

Her exclamation of pleasure at the sight of the brick and stone house pleased him. "Not like the really great houses," he said deprecatingly. "It was Tudor, as you see, first, then enlarged a century ago, the wings added, windows set in. It has been made comfortable, and I trust you will so find it." Offering an arm to each girl he led them up low steps into the entrance hall. "You have not had tea, I take it. Come to the Oak Room, do not change." He waved them toward a waiting housekeeper and the stairs on the right.

The rose and white room was up two flights and in one of the wings. A maid was unpacking their boxes feverishly and explaining they were not used to so many fine ladies and cook was shorthanded and all a-fluster. It was quicker to send her away and unpack themselves and then descend in search of the Oak Room.

A footman guided them to the ground floor and they found Lord Maleby standing in the center of a low, beamed room, one hand upraised, one finger pointing so it resembled a pistol. "This, as you see, is part of the original dwelling," he was intoning to several people looking obediently above them. "The timbers are the originals, all mid-sixteenth century I am told. They are the same in the solar, directly above the parlor where the ladies could sew and gossip in private. The panelling is also of oak and the same period. All this center portion of the house has been left untouched. The wings are imitation Adam, I am informed. But there, I am off on a hobby and keeping you from your tea. Here is my cousin, Mrs Cherington, to do the honors."

A handsome gray-haired lady entered on cue, bowing in several directions and went to the loaded table. The spread was lavish and Hester whispered it was no wonder cook was all a-fluster. Mr Meriney appeared and attached himself to Hester. Stephanie found herself listening to an older couple from Yorkshire who had come to inspect the Sussex sheep and ascertain if they would retain their particular qualities if transported to the moors. On her claiming complete ignorance they lost interest in her, and she could rise with them and move toward Airde at the front windows, circling a young couple listening raptly to Lord Maleby.

"Fascinating house," he remarked as she came beside him. "Forecourt is delightful." He nodded toward the beds of box and daffodils set in squares between white paths.

"Yes," agreed Lord Maleby complacently from behind them. "The house faces south, you see, an excellent location."

"One feels that the Channel lies just beyond that line of trees." Airde nodded to a low swell of a tree-topped hill.

"Not quite, not quite," Maleby told him, "but it is close, a matter of a mile or so. But we have water near at hand, our own cove there to the left below that grove, large enough for a small yacht for summer sailing."

"How very agreeable," Stephanie exclaimed. "I have never been sailing."

"Then you must come again in June. There is nothing like running before a good stiff breeze on a bright day." He gave way to the Yorkshire couple and Stephanie had no chance to speak to Airde.

Dinner was quite elaborate though Lord Maleby proclaimed it was only country fare to match the informality of country living, and this panelled and beamed room. There were a number of fish dishes that were delicious and mutton that, he said, was famous, and a surprising variety of creams. Over the coffee in a white and green salon on the first floor he announced that the ladies would be driven next morning to survey two quaint villages in the vicinity and the gentlemen would go riding. Though tables were set up for games no one seemed so inclined and the evening was short.

The villages, reached by narrow twisting roads, were charming, one, most unusual, of the local stone, which had pieces of dark flint embedded, and the other completely half-timbered and looking as it must have three hundred years before. Though pleased to see them and delighted by the curving hilly lanes, Stephanie felt it could not be held amusing entertainment for guests. She hoped Airde was doing better but he did not appear for lunch.

"Unpredictable man," Lord Maleby remarked at the table. "Suddenly said he had an old friend near Pevensey and would go to call and later have a look at the Roman fort. Do you not find Lord Airde unpredictable, Miss Langley?"

"I hardly know him well enough, my lord," she answered carelessly. "But I do know he has many interests," and gave him a guileless look and turned to Meriney.

With the other men Airde had inspected and admired the stables, approved of the horses, chosen his mount and followed his host on a lane that started north west. This would lead nowhere of interest. Abruptly he excused himself and at the next crossroads headed to the south, became lost in perverse lanes that twisted in every direction except the one they had first indicated, but eventually reached Bexhill. Here he stabled his horse at the White Hart on the edge of town and strolled down to the taverns at the water's edge. At the Royal Oak he bought a pint of ale and one for the only other occupant of the tap room who proclaimed that if he hadn't lost a leg at the Battle of the Nile he'd still be climbing to the yardarm and knew the Channel better than any captain. Learning a few names Airde wandered to another tavern, where he bought a round, listened and asked a few questions. He heard how easy it was to slip back and forth across the channel, which he knew already, and a little of the tides and currents and winds on that part of the coast. While most of the ships belonged to honest fishermen and smugglers, there were a number of yachts in tiny harbors or coves that the gentry owned or rented at times for pleasure cruises, on their own business.

He went on to admire three ships at anchor and

returned to his mount. After riding east and north a little he stopped at a lonely tavern where he shared fresh bread and butter and cheese and ale with the landlord and continued his ride. By a path through some woods he came out above a small bay and a white yacht. Two men were on deck and two more in a rowboat were warping the yacht around to face south. He waited in the cover of some trees until the ship was tied to the end of a long dock, wheeled, and was at Hawksdown well before tea.

In the Oak Room he found Stephanie, looking delicious in a muslin gown that matched the daffodils beyond the windows, on a sofa with Lord Maleby beside her. The sight annoyed Airde. Could that man, a widower of many years, have designs on Stephanie? He had no need to marry money, for he was held fat in the pockets, but a middle-aged widow should be more his style. Stephanie should be warned against him. But perhaps there was no need. Glancing around he saw Seddon and Meriney with Hester. Stephanie had implied quite definitely that her heart belonged to Seddon. Maleby would hold no appeal for her. Nevertheless, he advanced to the sofa and bowed.

"Deserter." Maleby wagged a finger at him amiably. "I trust you found your friend in good health."

"Excellent, thank you. And I stopped to look at the Roman fort at Pevensey, an amazing construction."

"Indeed. We have many fascinating spots along our coast." Maleby rose slowly. "Miss Langley, I look to continue our talk."

"It was most interesting to hear of your estate since

I know nothing of France." She knew Airde was watching her so she made her smile agreeable.

"With so delightful a listener one could not fail to produce some talk of interest," Lord Maleby said jovially and left them.

Airde rose, picked up her hand and brought her to her feet. "Come walk with me in the forecourt and admire the flowers." It was almost a command and though she made a moue for the sake of appearances she went willingly. As soon as they were down the steps he asked, "What was he talking about?"

"You would never guess. It seems that at the time of the truce a few years ago he obtained an estate of a dispossessed nobleman. He claims it is handsome. Somehow he has seen that it is kept in good repair and is eager for the war to end so he may inspect it. There is a park and a carp pond and the stables alone sound as large as Windsor."

"A strange subject, I agree. He has been making himself agreeable to you?"

"Is that so surprising?" She tilted her head on one side and looked at him from under her lashes. "You have favored me yourself, my lord, on occasion."

"Stop flirting with me. I am impervious, at the moment. He has been paying attentions?"

She would have liked to try another flirt but his face was so without expression she could tell he would not respond. "I must admit that since the Colesham ball he has paid me small attentions," she allowed. "It is not flattering that you had not noticed, sir."

"It isn't, is it? With apologies I do so confess. But there are so many gentlemen around you always . . ."

"Gammon." She had to laugh. "But you are forgiven for it is of small moment." She waved that away with one hand. "Are you not going to inform me of the reason behind that attack on you the other evening? I have been waiting for three whole days. And do not try to fob me off by saying it was common robbery, for at that time and place it could be no such thing."

"I would not try to mislead you, Miss Langley," he said solemnly, his expression now amused, "for I am aware I could not succeed. But I assure you I have no idea. They were lurking for any passerby, did not notice you, and when you cried out they fled."

She shook her head, she had thought of that herself and discarded the notion, but his look was so bland she knew he would advance no other notion. "I do not accept that but I will ask no more. But, oh, I have been waiting to tell you what you missed." She halted and burst out laughing and recounted the conversation of the two men from the first house. It was highly gratifying when he went into a whoop of laughter and suddenly looked younger than he had all day.

"Thank you for not revealing my name. Yes, I am acquainted with both of them and you can imagine my problem if they had learned I was involved and later we met. Also I must thank you again for getting me to Doria's and your care there. I am most grateful."

"Experience with my brother was helpful. And I felt so responsible." They had reached the end of the walk and she glanced over her shoulder. "Have you discovered any reason behind this visit? I cannot believe it was to advance Sir Andrew's position."

"Nor can I." He was serious again. "I have no clue.

We can only wait on events, a situation I dislike. Maleby must be up to some game of his own and I wish you were not here. I am furious at myself that I do not know what to warn you against or how to protect you. I am in a situation no gentleman could be proud of. But, then, I was not proud of myself the other night. Finding myself on the sidewalk cast me into the depths."

His rueful expression made her gurgle. "But you were at my feet, a unique position for you, though not of your own doing. But, sir, you can at least tell me if another packet of papers may be behind it all." She could not resist looking pleased at the idea.

"It might be. But stop looking so happy, like a kitten approaching a dish of cream. Nothing here has anything to do with you, remember that."

"But Lord Maleby is paying me some attention, sir."

"You said you did not care for him." He frowned.

"I do not like him at all, but since he is host I cannot avoid him entirely, as I would prefer. But surely I have nothing to fear."

"Of course not. But if there is ever any awkwardness just raise an eyebrow and I will be with you."

"That is if we can stay in sight of each other," she said skeptically, "but I will remember. Come, sir, it is time we went to change."

As they neared the steps Airde saw the heavy figure of Lord Maleby move away from a front window.

Chapter 13

THERE had been four more guests for dinner and others had come afterward for dancing in the long gallery on top of one of the wings. The people had been agreeable, though not very interesting, and the affair had passed off well. Though Lord Maleby brushed aside the compliments he received he was obviously pleased and in good spirits.

The guests had driven away and those remaining were moving from the front hall when he touched Stephanie's arm. "Come for a stroll with me and see my yacht. She is close at hand and under this full moon will make a pretty picture. I am eager to show her to you. I will get a cloak for you."

Stephanie moved and looked around for Airde, but could not find him. Maleby returned before she had decided how to refuse and flung a light cape over her shoulders. She drew back, not liking this at all but not seeing how to extricate herself. "You are kind, sir, but the grass will be wet and there is a breeze."

"There is a path and the breeze is just rising. Come. I do not often have a chance to show her to a lovely lady. You and the *Melusine* match and you should see her at her best."

Under his light words she knew was determination, and the hand which gripped her arm was strong. She could do nothing but allow herself to be guided to a path that turned left and skirted the lawn toward trees, while he expanded on the joys of sailing. By the time he was again comparing her and the ship they came to a break in the trees and looked down on the cove and the white yacht.

"So fortunate the cove is deep," Lord Maleby explained. "You see we can tie to the dock. Is she not a beauty?"

She was indeed handsome, larger than Stephanie had expected, shining in the moonlight. The water was dark beneath the trees on the opposite bank and a dancing sheen of light in the center made such an effective pattern that Stephanie exclaimed in admiration.

"I knew you could not fail to approve both the *Melusine* and her setting," Maleby said with satisfaction. "Now we will go down the steps and on board."

"Oh no, sir." Stephanie took a step backward. "That would not do at all. I am glad to have seen your *Melusine* but now we must return."

"You are coming aboard. I insist." That massive hand was holding her in place then urging her toward the steps. She tried to jerk her arm free but failed.

"Come, now." He was still speaking pleasantly. "I wish you to see how perfectly she is appointed. Would you prefer I have one of the sailors carry you?"

That thought was repugnant, and she found herself going down the steps, held to the descent by the heavy hand. It was a long flight of steps down, twenty-seven, she counted. She was afraid and determined not to show it. Then they were walking over the boards of the dock, up inclined cleated planks, through an opening in the rail and to the deck. The *Melusine* was larger than she had appeared from the top of the cliff, longer and broader, with two masts rocking a little, dark against the lighted sky.

"There will be time later to explore," Lord Maleby told her. "Now come see the main cabin," and he ushered her through a door into a brightly lit panelled room. Again Stephanie was surprised, though she knew little of ships, for it held a small desk and chair, a narrow table, three small armchairs and a serving buffet. There were red cushions in the chairs, long red cushions under the windows on each side and curtains to match and a Turkish carpet on the floor. The brass of the lamps was as bright as their flames. "Is it not handsome?" he asked proudly.

"It is indeed," Stephanie agreed. "Let us now return."

"It is a little warm in here," he began, took a step and twitched the cape from her shoulders. "We will have a brandy," he went on casually, "and there is a matter to settle and then we sail."

"Sail?" Her voice rose.

"Sail," and his smile was wide as he tossed the cloak in one corner. "I have decided that you not only match the *Melusine* but also the Chateau Malepin, so I am taking you with me. "In fact," and he gave a deep chuckle, "we will disappear together."

"You are out of your mind," Stephanie managed with dignity.

"Not at all, my dear. It is true I am using you as bait. But I have also a high opinion of your person and intelligence. I am convinced you will be a companion I will enjoy in many ways." The smile he sent her seemed both wolfish and triumphant.

She started for the door but he moved fast and caught her from behind, lifted her, and planted her in one of the chairs. "Stay there or I'll call a sailor to guard you." He turned away and shrugged out of his dinner coat and hung it on a peg between two nearby windows.

Again Stephanie was frightened. If she could get out of the door, off the ship, she could run faster than he could. It would take a little time to rouse the sailors to chase her. The long skirts were a handicap but she could hold them up. She looked around for something to use against him. On its peg, a slight rocking motion of the ship made the hanging coat swing open a little. In an inner pocket she glimpsed a white packet. Airde had allowed one such might be involved. She looked away and watched Maleby walk to the desk chair. Where was Airde? She need not be frightened, for he would rescue her. She folded her hands. Perhaps he needed more time . . . she should keep this dreadful man talking . . .

A silver tray held a decanter and two glasses. For the first time he noticed them, rose, poured and brought across one glass, presenting it with a flourish. "We will drink to our voyage and our journey," he announced. "You will enjoy it all, I promise you, and also your stay at my château."

"But how can I; sir, without the proper clothes?" She gave him a coy look. "This is so unexpected . . . You gave little indication of your interest."

"I had little at first," he acknowledged condescendingly. "Then you were a guest of Lady Diana Inverskaid, which increased my interest. I have become quite taken with what I have seen of you on this visit and decided you would suit me admirably. Take a sip, now, to our future."

She sipped, felt the strengthening warmth, and thought of something else. Lolling at ease in the opposite armchair, he was watching her narrowly. "There is still the problem of my clothes," she said, as airily as she could. "We would both be vastly bored if I had no change of costume for days."

"At this time, it will only be three or four days. But I pride myself on being foresighted. Your wardrobe should be on board any moment, and should be sufficient."

His words increased her feeling of menace but she managed to say lightly, "Foresighted indeed! But you said I was a bait?"

"Obviously. For Airde. He will follow you. The trail is plain for him."

"He goes on the journey with us?" Her surprise was genuine.

"Only part way, not beyond mid-channel. He should be here any moment." He tossed back the rest of his brandy. "Oh, yes. He will come aboard and my men will take care of him." He stood up, a stalwart figure in his white shirt and satin vest embroidered in green to match his evening breeches.

"You planned this from the beginning, when you invited Lord Airde and the rest of us?" She was still surprised.

"From the moment I picked up some dispatches, and right from under his nose, too. I do not underestimate him and I knew he would discover and place the loss. Later, more impetuously than is my custom, I hoped to remove him by another means, more simple, that would have saved me trouble. When that failed I had my original scheme to fall back on. So fortunate—it brought you to me."

"So it was you behind the attack on Lord Airde the other evening."

"Of course. But the stupid oafs thought once he was down he could be finished off. But you screamed, two men appeared, my two fell into a panic and ran. They were adequately punished."

"But . . ." she began.

"But," he picked up smoothly, "their failure brought your visit and so I now count on certain pleasures ahead." He looked her up and down appreciatively.

She ignored all he had said for she had her own plan. She rose and stepped over to return her glass to the tray. "It is a most handsome cabin," she murmured, moved toward the windows that gave on the shore, then backed halfway across the space. "Is that a figure or a shadow on the steps?" She pointed as she asked.

As Maleby hurried to peer she backed to the hanging coat, felt it, found the pocket and packet, twitched it out and held it behind her. She backed still further until she felt the sill of the open window, raised the packet and dropped it outside on the deck. It could wait there for Airde. She was four steps away by the time Maleby made an irritated gesture.

"I see nothing," he growled, "but it will not be long. His interest in you is so strong he will come, he believes, to save you. I had to make very sure he would come for there is the possibility he does not suspect me. And no one will know where either of you have gone." His smile seemed to her positively wolfish. "Your disappearance will be a mystery for the gossips."

"Along with your own, sir?" she inquired quickly.

"Oh no. I shall return in a few days. I took you out for a moonlight sail, you see, and the *Melusine* was blown out into the Channel and somehow in the confusion caused by the storm both you and Airde were blown overboard and in spite of greatest efforts could not be saved. In the process we drifted too close to the French shore and had to conceal the ship near Fécamp until we could sail back. It will make an engrossing story. I will be desolated of course and something of a hero."

"What a program! You have it all worked out to a fivepence."

"Naturally. And my crew is extremely well paid, so do not think to appeal to their sympathies."

"But you said earlier we would go to your château." She gestured as if in bewilderment.

"Ultimately. I will leave you there—it is below Evreux—on my way to Paris, visit you on my return and come again—later." He looked to the moonwashed steps, shrugged, and sat down behind the desk, and turned to watch Stephanie. "You are cool and brave, Miss Langley. You are not disturbed by your coming— voyage?"

"My abduction? I suppose I should be flattered. But I see no need to work myself into a fret because of an impossibility." To show she was at ease she improperly crossed one knee over the other, pulled up the fan that dangled from her wrist and opened it.

"You are trusting too much to Airde," he sneered, and lifted his head at the sound of steps. Through the door a sailor and Meriney dragged an inert figure by its feet and left it on the floor. Stephanie's heart seemed to halt. Airde had worn black that evening, Sir Andrew dark blue. She jumped up to run to the figure, and saw it wore blue and the hair was light.

"Sit down, Miss Langley," Maleby ordered, and told the sailor he could go. "Now," the big man towered over Meriney, "what is the meaning of this?"

Meriney looked surprised at the tone. "He followed Airde so I followed him, for of course I was coming here anyway. By the woods he stopped, uncertain I suppose, so I got ahead of him and across the dock before he reached the stairs. When he came up the gangplank I hit him. The sailor came running and helped me pull him in here."

"How could you hit him?" Stephanie demanded hotly. "He is taller than you."

Meriney laughed, and brought up his right hand to show a pistol. "Why, with the butt of this, Miss Langley. I was above him and could lean over and hold him as he fell and the sailor arrived." He faced Maleby. "Since he had come so far I am sure you wish to keep him so there can be no word of Airde's—fate."

"You are sure Lord Airde is on board?"

"He must be, for he was well ahead of this one." He gestured and lowered the pistol. "The sailors will take care of him."

Stephanie looked at the windows again. They were too small for her to get through. There was only the one door. If she could get out, create a diversion . . . She began to edge toward the door.

"No, Miss Langley, you cannot escape," Maleby said. "You are the bait, remember, to bring Airde here, and you could not, in any case."

"But where is he?" Meriney burst out excitedly. "If he has evaded the sailors you and I can handle him. We have guns and I have a dagger . . ."

"Which I trust you will have no occasion to use," an amused voice said behind him as Airde came through the door and seized Meriney from behind by his neckpiece. Meriney gave a choking gasp. He was pulled back a little, the pistol was removed from his hand and he was pushed forward into the room. Lord Airde remained in the doorway.

"So the bait worked," Lord Maleby gloated.

"Oh, yes. I could not leave Miss Langley to whatever plans you may have had for her. You did not need to involve her. I would have come anyway." He turned a half circle and bowed to Stephanie. "I trust you have not been inconvenienced, ma'am." He turned back and his gaze fell on Seddon. "Poor chap. I hope you did not hit him too hard, Mr Meriney."

"It was a little awkward, I grant," Meriney acknowledged, and backed up a little. "I regretted that it was necssary. But where are the sailors?"

"The three, plus the cook, are in the hold and quite safe. The captain is locked in his cabin. Quiet surprise can accomplish a great deal."

"Evidently." Maleby paused. "You said you would have come anyway?"

"How could you doubt? Oh, I see," and the lean face lit with amusement, "You were not completely convinced I had sufficient intelligence to interpret the warmth of the seals you had replaced on the packet. But, my good man, once you had the ship turned to face the Channel your intentions were obvious. And I learned enough of winds and currents this morning to clinch them. I could not allow you to escape. I could have followed you to France, if necessary." He was quite matter-of-fact, stating something self-evident.

"He *is* going to France," Stephanie broke in excitedly. "He told me, to near Fécamp, then to that château, then to Paris and in a few days back here."

"What an elaborate schedule!" Airde drawled.

"Yes." Meriney straightened proudly. "And I go with him to Paris and have the honor of presenting dispatches of the greatest importance to the emperor himself and in gratitude he will return to me my own estate. Lord Maleby has promised me that will come about."

"What a—bait," Airde gave the young man a look of compassion. "No, Maleby, do not reach for that drawer of your desk that holds your pistol. We have more to discuss."

"You had better be quick. The captain will not be out of action for long," Maleby advised with equal coolness.

Meriney had obviously been following his own line of thought. "The dispatches, my lord. You have them safe?"

Maleby nodded. "In my coat pocket over there."

Ignoring Airde, Meriney ran to the coat that was moving a little on its peg. He felt in every pocket and turned, his face stricken. "It is not here."

"No?" Maleby gave him a wide smile. "It was. How unfortunate for you it is not there now."

Desolation crumpled Meriney's face. He groaned and buried his face in the coat.

"No one is allowed to stand in my way." Maleby actually chuckled. "Much less a pretty lady, who has evidently had her own ideas."

His face was not pleasant. Stephanie looked away. What could she do to help Airde? A movement caught her attention. Sir Andrew had rolled over on his back and was at one side of the door, but his eyes were still closed.

"Not good form to frighten a lady," Airde reproved. "Don't worry, my dear. It will be all right."

As he spoke a loop of rope fell over his head and shoulders down to his elbows, was pulled tight and snaked around his legs and knotted, and the pistol was jerked from his hand. "Is this the man you warned us against, my lord?" A tall grizzled man with an air of some authority held the end of the rope. Airde did not move.

"Excellent, captain," Maleby approved loudly. "Knew I could trust you."

"Yes, sir. Took me by surprise, he did, threw me in my cabin and locked the door. Took me a few minutes to get out. Went around the deck and found this below the porthole, saw him in here and went for a rope, not being sure what you wished done with him." From the pocket of his jacket he produced the packet. Meriney gave a shout and leaped to take it from his hands.

Ignoring him, Maleby looked with a slow smile of pleasure at Airde. "You did exactly right, captain. Thank you." He strode from behind the desk. "You have given me an unexpected opportunity for something I have long desired." He halted in front of Airde and slapped him, first on one cheek and then on the other. Still smiling, he drew back a clenched fist and aimed at Airde's face, but Airde bent to one side and the fist only landed on his shoulder, hardly staggering him.

"You're a peasant and a coward," Stephanie called out from her chair.

Maleby paused, shrugged, and went back behind his desk. "I've always hated you, Airde," he said almost conversationally. "You were always blocking me. But we have time ahead to even old scores."

"No scores on my part," Airde told him quite cheerfully. "Never thought you worth considering. Do you feel better now?"

"What are your orders, my lord?" the captain asked stolidly as Maleby's clenched hand dropped on the desk.

"We sail for France," Meriney shouted, waving the packet above his head. "France—Paris—my reward for this. You cannot deny me my right."

"Do not be stupid." Maleby glanced at him a little wearily. "You have no right. You do not go to Paris."

"But you promised me." The young man halted, aghast. "You have used me, my friends, the information they sent me for three years. I helped you. I have the dispatches and will take them myself, I, Philippe de Meriney, to the emperor."

"You will not." The flat decisive voice halted Meriney.

"Don't you see?" Airde broke in. The red marks of the blows stood out on his cheeks. "There's no need for those papers to go to Napoleon, even though they outline Wellington's plans and needs for the next campaign. You doubtless helped him, but I wager Lord Maleby copied much of the original. Undoubtedly he has an excellent memory and can repeat all the essentials."

A pleased look crossed the heavy face. "How clever of you, my lord."

"Which," Airde went on, "you cannot, Meriney. He does not need you any longer."

"Of course," Maleby agreed. Ignoring the captain standing behind Airde, Meriney clutching the packet and murmuring to himself, Seddon on the floor, Stephanie watching from her chair, he spoke only to Airde. "You are the only one who knows I have had Wellington's letters in my possession and time to read and copy them. I regret I was so careless as to return the packet to you before the seals I had replaced had time to cool. You might not have suspected what had happened."

"I assure you I would have," Airde said gently, "knowing something of your character."

Maleby ignored that also. "Since your chief delivered them to the p.m. the following morning and then left for Derbyshire, you have had no chance to confess to him your carelessness nor my involvement. You are my only danger, so I arranged this little incident on the *Melusine*. It would have been better," he added, "if my men had eliminated you successfully the other evening."

"Undoubtedly, for you," Airde agreed cordially.

"He's going to put you overboard in mid-Channel," Stephanie called across.

"Plans can be changed if necessary. But, no matter. I go to Paris and return quickly, until the war is over."

"And Wellington and our English soldiers?"

The heavy shoulders shrugged. "He and his men take their chances, they are no concern of mine. The emperor will know how to deal with our army."

"And my friends here?"

Maleby shrugged again. "The lady accompanies me to France and remains there at my pleasure. You and the stupid Seddon will be lost overboard and there can hardly be an inquiry. Since Meriney threatens to become a nuisance he will be lost with you."

In the moment of silence the captain asked for his orders.

Maleby came back from contemplating something pleasant. "Why, leave him here." He opened his desk drawer and brought out a pistol and cocked it, leaving it on top of the desk. "Go and release the crew. Cast off and head for the Channel. Do not yet raise the sails, the wind and current will carry us offshore."

As he finished Seddon gave a roll, crashed into Airde and kicked violently at the captain. Airde flung himself back and knocked the captain off his feet. Seddon rolled again until he was lying on top of the man.

Stephanie ran to Meriney. "You said you had a dagger. Give it to me." As he pulled it from his pocket she snatched it and ran to Airde to hack at the rope around his arms. As it fell he seized the dagger and bent to saw on the rope on his legs, muttering to her to go back to her chair. With a glance at his progress and at Seddon, who had a hand on the captain's throat, she went. Even as she did Airde had twisted and taken the pistol from the captain's jerking hand. The rope fell away. Meriney jumped and picked up the dagger from the floor and retreated so his back was against the wall, his face bemused and tragic. Maleby watched.

"Too bad one shot couldn't dispose of all of us," Airde observed as he straightened. "Stay where you are, Seddon. We want the captain *hors de combat*." The man was heaving, striving to throw off the weight on top of him. "Better choke him, Seddon. And now, Maleby, what next?"

His lordship looked at the pistol in Airde's hand and

down at his own lying on the desk. "It would avail either of us little if we shot each other," he observed thoughtfully.

"And I would not miss."

Maleby shot him a quick glance. "Nor would I."

"At this distance we would both be dead," Airde pointed out. "That is obvious."

"A waste of good men," Maleby began. "Suppose we forget the whole thing, Airde. The captain will release the crew and we will slip out of the cove. You and your friends return to the house after a midnight stroll. Meriney I will settle with later. No one will know of this—incident."

"Except the emperor—and Wellington and his men," Airde pointed out gently. "Do you really think I would let you escape?"

"I could make it very much worth while for all . . ."

Meriney had been watching them both, his head turning as each spoke. "I no longer trust you," he began slowly, looking to his left, his left hand clutching the packet. "You said you would settle with me. I do not care for that."

"Perhaps you were unwise to trust me in the beginning," Maleby told him carelessly, his eyes on Airde. "It is evident I have no further use for you and cannot let you interfere with my visit to Paris."

"So. It is from your own mouth you condemn yourself." Meriney shook his head as if bewildered. "You tell me my years, my work have been in vain. Your sacred promise you break. Me you cast aside and will settle with. I know how you settle with people." He paused, his breath coming in gasps.

"I fear you were deceived by a very wicked man," Airde said sympathetically.

"Yes. Completely. Now he would rob me of my hope, my future, my life." He took a step toward the desk, his right hand going into the pocket of his jacket.

"You have no one to blame but yourself," Maleby told him sternly. "You were stupid. You could think of nothing but your estate. You were useful, I admit, but you are no longer." His hand crept toward his pistol. Airde's eyes narrowed as he watched both men, and he raised his pistol.

Meriney crept forward again. "So, *canaille,* you betray your own country, my trust, your promises."

Maleby stepped back from the desk, pistol in hand. "Stay back," he ordered hoarsely.

Meriney was at the side of the deck. "You shall not profit by your betrayals," he screamed and leaped forward, the dagger high, and plunged it with all his strength into Maleby's chest. At the same moment Maleby raised his pistol and shot into Meriney's chest. The two sagged forward and fell together at the far corner of the desk.

"How very convenient," Airde said slowly. "Don't look, Stephanie."

He went and knelt by the two men and when he rose the packet was in his hand. Shoving paper and pistol into his pocket he returned and knelt by Seddon. "Can you get up? You can ease your hold on the captain's throat now. I am sure he would be glad to have you do so."

Seddon waited, removed his hand and struggled to rise. Airde caught his arm and eased him into a chair. "It's all right now, captain," he said over his shoulder. "Would you take a brandy and pour one for my friend? You could both use it."

"Indeed, sir. A strong man, your friend." The captain got to his knees and pulled himself up by the door, shook himself, felt his throat and made a grimace and poured the brandy. One he downed quickly, the other he brought to Airde, who held it to Seddon's lips. Seddon sipped and nodded and sipped again. "What . . .?" he began and took the glass.

"Later." Airde turned to the captain, who was taking a second. "You will release the crew from the hold and take the ship out as planned," he ordered crisply. "When well out from shore you will return to this cabin. The two men behind the desk are dead. I suggest you get very well into the Channel and get rid of them in deep water. Then the ship is yours."

"It's mine anyway," the captain grinned. "His late Lordship rented it when he had a mind to, for various reasons, and acted like it was his own, but 'twarn't."

"Splendid. Good luck with her. I trust he paid you in advance for this trip."

"Always had that done, sir, not trusting the gentry. Did you kill them? From where I was, so to speak, I couldn't see what happened."

"No, I did not. They killed each other, as you will see, as they were practically body to body when they shot and stabbed."

"They didn't like each other nohow, so I'm not surprised. We're well rid of them, though the young chap had pleasant ways. His lordship was a nasty piece of goods and a devil when crossed. I'll see they're never found, sir."

"Good." Airde held out his hand. "And we don't need to know each other's names."

"Right you are, sir. Now I'll give you a hand ashore with your friend."

They helped Seddon to his feet and out the door. "Come along, Stephanie," Airde called over his shoulder.

Meekly she followed.

Chapter 14

WEARILY Stephanie plodded across the short grass toward the lights of Hawkswood. Though she had moved little in the past two hours she had been holding herself so tensely that all her muscles ached. It had been an effort to hold up her dress and mount the stairs and it was one now to avoid small hussocks and stones made visible by the bright moonlight, since evening shoes were not made for rough walking. Ahead the two men were moving slowly, Seddon's arm across Airde's shoulders. Poor dear Sir Andrew, she thought, and that took her back to the scene on the *Melusine*. Maleby must have been mad, for only madness would make an Englishman turn traitor, madness or greed, or both. Meriney had lost his control and his mind in those last minutes. She should be more shocked than she was, perhaps, as she avoided a hump of grass, but as a soldier's daughter she could only feel it was right and proper for traitors to die. But it was just as well she had not had a clear view of the killings. She halted just before colliding with the two figures.

They had stopped and Seddon had lowered his arm. "I'm all right," he muttered. "Must walk into the house."

"Good." Airde kept hold of one arm. "We won't be there for long. There'll be no hue and cry for Maleby for a few days, he must have left some word with his steward. But we will leave at early light, with due apologies written for Mrs Cherington."

Stephanie gave cry. "My clothes!. That man said he had them removed to the ship. I can't go to London like this and abandon my clothes."

Both men gave her a long look as she faced them, curls tumbled around her head, shoulders and arms white in the moonlight, sequins on the airy dress twinkling. "You look charming," Seddon said heavily.

"But you are right about your problem," Airde agreed.

"Yes, yes." Stephanie turned her head and felt herself begin to sway with the motion. She was caught, steadied and picked up into Airde's arms.

"You poor child," he said softly. "I'll take you to the house and go back for your things."

After the first startled moment she found herself snuggling against his chest, hearing the beat of his heart, feeling the comfort of his arms. To explain that improper snuggle she let herself go limp. All too soon they were in the empty hall and the Oak Room and she was being set carefully in a chair. "Can you climb the stairs?" he asked.

Before she could answer there was a little cry and Hester was running toward her. "I stayed awake. I was so concerned. All is well?" She saw Seddon collapsing on a sofa. "Oh no, not well."

"We trust it is nothing serious," Airde reassured her. "You might put a cold compress on the spot where he was hit. I am going to the ship for Miss Langley's boxes." He was out the door.

Hester paused in her flight for the compress. "Your boxes? But they are in your room. Nothing has been touched."

Without thinking how quickly she had recovered, Stephanie sped out the door, the hall, to the forecourt. Airde was moving quickly toward the trees. "Airde," she called, her voice sounding to her like a marsh bird. "Airde," and began to run after him, regardless of pebbles on the walk or unevenness of the lawn. At her third call he stopped, reversed and came back toward her. By then she was running faster and could not halt and landed squarely against his chest.

It was a moment before she could catch her breath and gasp, "Don't go. That man lied. Hester says my boxes have not been taken away at all."

"So you came to spare me the walk." He held her another moment then dropped his arms. "I confess I am glad not to have to make that visit."

The moon was still high. A small breeze brushed by them to stir the grass and then the tops of the trees. Airde's face was all planes and shadows, forehead and hair lighted, eyes and hollows of cheeks hidden, wide well-cut mouth and chin clear. Stephanie felt her heart move unaccountably at the unexpected portrait. She felt there was no hurry to return to the house at once, and remembered her oversight.

"I have not thanked you for saving me from that man," she faltered. "I am deeply grateful. He was dreadful beyond belief, and I knew I would be treated abominably." She turned her face up to his and hoped he could read her sincerity behind her words.

"I was happy I could," he said lightly and his mouth curved at the corners. "It fortunately coincided with my duty. The ending, as I said, was convenient as I had not thought it would be."

His smile and the lightness of his voice annoyed her. How could he treat her rescue so casually, unless it meant nothing to him? So she had better show it meant nothing to her. Her voice took on the flutter she had not used for a long time. "Of course I am glad it amused you, that it was merely an entertainment. Doubtless rescuing damsels in distress is an ordinary occurence in your life. I have been given to understand there have been so many romantic episodes in your past that there is nothing new left to capture your fancy." She moved back and finding her fan still dangling from her wrist began to wave it. "And how unfortunate Maleby did not need to use me as bait after all. You would have been spared the extra obligation and my nerves a frightful *crise.*"

"Stop it, Stephanie," he told her amiably. "You do not need to go fluttery again to show you resent having been second in my thoughts. Maleby underestimated me, thinking he needed a bait to bring me to him. Of course I would have gotten around to bringing you ashore, when what I came for was finished. And your nerves did not suffer a *crise* so don't try to raise that breeze. You were most admirably cool and collected throughout, and quick to get that dagger to me, and cut the rope. I was gratified, but not surprised, that you did not go into even mild hysterics."

The praise was pleasing, and she felt deserved, but she fastened on another point. "It was evident you had something more important on your mind than saving me from kidnapping and ravishing."

"Of course." It was a flat statement that permitted no question. "My duty came first, no matter what I found on the yacht. I could not let Maleby himself get to France and pour out all he had read of—our military intentions. Maleby thought I was merely after the copy he had made and which he could throw to the dogs, along with Meriney. You heard what was said, so stop being perverse."

"You would have killed him?" she asked with awe.

"That was my intention. But I must confess I am exceedingly glad that I did not have to. I prefer to kill, if I have to, only in combat. I told you once that I detest violence. But this is a waste of a good moon. Drop that fan, for, regardless of all my resolutions, I am going to kiss you and I do not want that thing poking me in the eye."

Stephanie dropped the fan, eyes widening. "That is not proper . . ." she began and found herself crushed in his arms and a very firm mouth on hers. After a long moment it was murmuring that she was beautiful and wonderful and she found she was answering happily.

There came a shout from the open door and steps on the path. "Airde, where are you? We must arrange for tomorrow."

"Blast. I had a lot more to say and do," Airde muttered and dropped his arms, then caught her elbow to steady her.

Stephanie wished she could clutch at him, stay in his arms, be kissed again. Of course any arms would be comforting at such a time but his had felt trustworthy as well as strong. And his kisses almost overpowering . . . But he was turning toward the house and moving her with him. Seddon was approaching slowly. In the full moon he was as beautiful as ever and she gazed at him almost bemused, then, conscious of Airde's glance, dropped her eyes.

"Glad she caught you." Seddon stopped. "Came to see. We must set up our departure."

"Quite right." Airde removed his hand. "But you are in no condition to walk down to the stables. Escort Miss Langley to the house and I will see to everything." He gazed at them as Seddon held out his arm and Stephanie looked back and nodded before placing her hand."

"You both will have little time to pack and get some sleep." Seddon looked worried. "I should have gone, you know, but he manages everything so effortlessly."

"Yes," Stephanie whispered in agreement and remembered the kiss that had been managed so well. Matching her gait to Seddon's slow pace they reached the open door and Hester.

Airde's easy management was evident, for the coach and the horses drew up at a side door at six and in five minutes boxes were stowed and they were moving down the driveway. An hour later they stopped for breakfast of ale and bread and cheese at a hedgerow inn. Airde assured them he had left a very proper note for Mrs Chering which also conveyed their regrets to Lord Maleby that they had been summoned away so unceremoniously. Stephanie had been watching Seddon across the table as he ate hesitantly and his eyes kept closing. She caught Airde's eye and looked to Seddon and then they were outside by the coach.

"It's the box seat for you, my man," he told Seddon. "You'll be nigh falling off your horse in a moment."

"It's my head," Seddon said unsteadily, "and my shoulder, but I can manage."

"You'll do no such thing," Stephanie asserted indignantly. "You will be down on the road. You will go in the coach and I will ride on the box seat." She gave Airde, who had an odd look, a beguiling smile. "It is something I have long wished to do, you must understand, and here is my chance."

"It is not proper, Stephanie," Hester protested.

"Pooh." Stephanie tossed her head. "Who will see and what do I care anyway? Sir Andrew is quite unfit to remain upright." Seddon had wilted a little and the footman was summoned to help place him in a corner of the coach with cushions around him. When Hester was settled his head fell on her shoulder which, she said in her soft voice, did not incommode her in the least and would make the ride more comfortable for him.

"Welcome aboard, miss." The Irish-looking coachman beamed at Stephanie as she was placed and Airde threw a light rug across her knees. " 'Tain't often I have beauty riding beside me."

"Coming too rare, Mahon. You know you pick up every pretty girl on the road when you're alone," Airde laughed.

Mahon chuckled. "And glad they are to have me, sir. But this is beauty and quality and I'll look out for her, never fear."

"Look after the horses first and move them along a little faster if you can." While they discussed where to halt, where to change horses, a possible change of road, Stephanie untied the ribbons of her bonnet and leaned down to throw it in the coach door.

Her shoulder was seized roughly. "Never lean down from the box seat," Airde said harshly. "You could fall on your head, something might frighten the horses and make them start . . . Here." He took the bonnet and tossed it through the window. "I've a mind to put you inside on the floor."

"Oh, no. You could not be so cruel. I promise to remember." She gave him another appealing smile. "Besides, we are wasting time while you are being unkind."

His mood changing in a flash, he laughed and they started.

It was as exhilarating to ride on the box seat as Stephanie had always imagined. Though she knew it was not in reality very high above the ground it was higher than any other spot she had occupied since her tree climbing days. She looked down on a wagon cart they passed and felt vastly superior. The view over the fields was wider than from the coach and she could gaze upward at treetops, clouds and the bluest of skies. As they trotted through a village she felt sorry for the few folk walking on the road. Once again in the country she sniffed the air, sure it was more fresh from her seat than from the ground, and certainly the breeze was more refreshing. A bird flew by them, quite close, and she clapped her hands and looked at Mahon and laughed out loud. When Airde suddenly appeared at her side, for there was space for his horse, she laughed again and threw out her arms. "It's all so beautiful," she cried. "I could dance and sing with joy."

Watching her vivid face Airde laughed with her while Mahon promised if she did any of that he'd guarantee to hold in the horses until she finished.

She protested at being lifted down when they stopped in late morning, though she was glad enough to have tea and hot bread under a green arbor. Here was a pause in what had seemed like a headlong rush of events, and mysteries. Seddon was sitting with his head on one hand taking his tea by the spoonful and Hester was trying to hide that she was watching him anxiously. Airde was gazing into a distance of dipping fields and hills and groves of trees. There would soon be no chance to talk, Stephanie was sure, so she might as well try to find out some things now.

She reached over and touched Airde's arm. "Come back from wherever you are," she coaxed, "and tell me more of what happened and why."

He moved his head and laughter was in his eyes. "I was wondering how long your curiosity would be held in check. What do you wish to know?"

She had not stopped to order her thoughts so began with the most obvious. "Why did Lord Maleby want us down here? Was it truly just to do away with you? Why should he want me as a bait, as he said, which was quite ridiculous, of course."

"I should have remembered that a simple question and answer would never suffice for you." He gave a mock sigh. "There is much we'll not know, ever, and much you do not need to know. But you have heard a little and deserve to share a little more. I told you, and you saw, that a packet of utmost importance was involved. It was involved by my carelessness. Maleby obtained it, and it gave him an opportunity for a really great coup, a triumph, a reward for his years of patience and all his private activities. It was up to me, as I said, to make sure he did not achieve his triumph. From the circumstances he could be sure I would know very soon that he had it. I was a danger to him. He thought very fast. He knew where Lord Fanning-thorpe would be when I took the recovered papers to him, and because of the distinguished company I would not be able to speak to him, and that he was leaving early for Derbyshire. So Maleby had to get me somewhere logical where I could be disposed of neatly and mysteriously in case questions arose. What better spot than his own place? So the very prompt invitation. But an invitation to me alone would not do at all. So you were included, he probably even then had a use for you in mind—and Seddon and Hester to conceal his purposes. Do you follow? I regret the explanation is involved but I cannot think how to simplify it."

Stephanie frowned a little. "You are very clear. I think I understand. Since only you knew he had seen those papers he had to make sure you would never tell, for if you did his word might not have more weight than yours." Seddon's name had brought up another mystery. "Why did he have Sir Andrew making those weekly trips to Mrs Riffton's?"

"I cannot be sure. He prided himself on being a very farsighted man who planned ahead. It is my guess he long had some scheme in mind and knew Seddon would never suspect anything. The papers that were put in his pockets were quite genuine, from spies in France, whom he maintained on his own, and recruited in part through Meriney. They gave him additional bits of information with which he could impress his colleagues and enhance his own position. If anything went wrong Seddon was the perfect scapegoat. I abstracted three from Seddon so I know that part. What Meriney carried were questions, instructions, rumors and a little real information, all to sustain Maleby's importance with his French correspondents and an undoubtedly high man in Paris."

"Once more, you are admirably clear, my lord, and

I am more than satisfied," Stephanie approved. "Thank you."

He gave a deep sigh. "So gratifying to have pleased you, my dear. It can be so difficult."

She refused to join in his funning; there was more to learn. "Then all of those errands Maleby sent Sir Andrew on, to look for papers, I mean, was to make it easier to blame him if need arose?"

"That is my belief; a lamb to throw to the wolves. Maleby was an intriguer. He could have used Seddon any way he needed and so plausibly—a poor officer, easy access to information the French would pay for, who would have believed Seddon's denials? Of course those errands were false, but they could have been twisted to appear his own idea."

"And you were pretending?"

"Not entirely. Various kinds of papers are sometimes missing. Also I wished to keep track of Seddon to see if he found anything, and perhaps discover something of Maleby's activities. But we are free of all that now. Seddon is not well. Let us be off."

Stephanie agreed gladly, for the man did look ill, but protested again when Airde informed her she was to ride inside for a while to keep her from the heat of the sun. He contrived to have Seddon placed on the floor with his head and shoulder surrounded by cushions and pointed out he would neither know or care if the girls placed their feet on his legs when they were weary of sitting in a curl. Stephanie was in the process of telling Hester of the joys of riding on the box when she found her eyes closing and she was into a nap. There was a stop for a country tea and after that she insisted on returning to the box. This time her stay was shorter for they were entering larger villages and Airde said severely he would not have his reputation ruined by his coach seen with a hatless female nonchalantly riding with the coachman.

"Pooh. Your reputation can stand much more than that trifle," she told him airily. Though he grinned he removed her firmly. She admitted to herself she was really just as glad and glad when they reached Montague Street and could climb to her room, leaving Airde to explain the early return.

Evidently he blamed that on an accident, cause unspecified, to Sir Andrew, which Cousin Doria deplored as well as the brevity of the visit and the long drives. She showed no interest in the people encountered and remarked she had never cared for Lord Maleby and realized they had only gone because dear Sir Andrew was on his staff. Since Hester had not been on the yacht and was only told Sir Andrew had somehow been injured and evinced no interest in Airde's explanation, being occupied with trying to persuade Sir Andrew to take some tea, Stephanie had no one to talk with about it all. She found herself missing Airde and looking for him to call, and dwelling on his aquiline face and hazel eyes that could be cool, amused, warm, or suddenly ablaze. There was also the attraction of his long figure and the calm certainty with which he met and managed any situation. Except one, and her breath caught always at that memory. There in the moonlight at Hawksdown he had not been calm and cool. But, she decided, it must have been the moonlight that carried him above himself.

She stayed in the house two afternoons so as to be sure not to miss him in case he called. All that arrived was a note to Cousin Doria telling her that Sir Andrew had a broken collarbone and a slight concussion but was recovering so well Airde felt he could leave town for a few days. They would call on his return. Which was all unsatisfactory except, as Hester pointed out, for the good news that Sir Andrew was improving. Stephanie allowed she also rejoiced and reminded herself that of course she had loved Sir Andrew from first sight, though she did not think of him quite so frequently now. And Airde she would dismiss from her thoughts, for she did not know what to make of him, except that he was always mysterious, which was aggravating.

It was undeniably comforting that Lord Warebrook was constant in his attentions. He was always amusing and the best of company and she enjoyed the outings he provided and his escort to opera and balls. He gave no hint of any serious intentions, but that was a relief for she could not guess what she would respond. They dealt exceedingly well, but would that be sufficient for the rest of her life? Would there be absorbing depths to his mind and character for her to explore? Did they have really the same tastes in addition to the pursuit of light-hearted pleasure? Did country life hold appeal for him as well as the gaiety of a season? She endeavored to learn, but he turned the subject aside with a laugh. Yet it was most evident he enjoyed her company. So, she told herself, they had not been acquainted for a sufficient length of time to really know each other, and, as a well brought up girl, she should not strive to look ahead. And who could tell what might happen? And surely she was proving to herself she did not need Airde's presence for full enjoyment of London and its society.

Chapter 15

IT was nine days after their return from Hawksdown that the footman brought at lunchtime a note asking permission for Lord Airde and Sir Andrew Seddon to call that afternoon at four.

"It is positively rag-mannered not to give us more time between note and arrival," objected Cousin Doria. "But Airde can be impetuous on occasion," and she sent back a note assuring him the gentlemen would be welcome.

At ten minutes before four the three ladies were waiting in the pleasant green and white drawing room. Long windows looked over the garden and at one end rose a delicate white fireplace adorned by garlands of plump putti which Stephanie thought singularly inappropriate. At four the gentlemen, meticulously garbed, strode into the room and bowed. One glance at their stern, closed faces and Stephanie was sure something unpleasant was in the wind.

"Dear Doria." Airde advanced and bowed again. "I am convinced that you and some of your bosom-bow friends would enjoy a drive this sunny afternoon to be followed by a visit to Gunther's. So I have brought my barouche for you to use as you wish and sent word that the ices are to be unlimited in number."

"Dear Esham," Doria cooed, after a first startled glance, "so like you to think one can pick up friends without notice for a jaunt of any kind."

"But you always have an inclination for any entertainment at a moment's notice." He smiled winningly. "I am persuaded your friends must match you. Surely you can find two or three who would enjoy the excursion."

"And being seen in the Airde vehicle," she said a little scathingly. "However, I believe I can locate two who will forgive such informality and be free to accompany me." She rose. "Such a charming way of getting rid of a chaperon." She inclined her head, nodded to Sir Andrew, glanced at the girls and laughed. "Whatever is eating at them there is no guessing, but I trust you will weather the storm with flying colors, my loves, and will tell me all, or rather all you are permitted, on my return." Halfway to the door she paused. "If he gets in his high stirrups just pay him no heed," she advised and laughed again.

"I call that high-handed beyond endurance," sputtered Stephanie.

Airde gave her a cold glance. "Why? She enjoys a drive with her friends and being seen at Gunther's. What better way could I get rid of her and yet give her some pleasure?"

How irritating it was that so often he could stir her up, as her nurse used to say. "You always have the most plausible explanations and excuses for whatever you wish to do."

"You must blame that on my Foreign Office training," he answered blandly.

Though that might have been a promising trail to follow, she had a more important crow to pick with him. "You have been away," and her tone was more tart than she intended.

He raised his eyebrows in that haughty fashion he had when answering something that was out of line. "As I wrote in my note," he agreed equably. "And to forestall your next question, which you would have no business asking but probably would anyway, I went down to Kent. Rye has a delightful and comfortable inn. You must try it some day. And, yes, I ascertained that Hawksdown is closed except for caretakers. Nothing has been heard from Lord Maleby, and his man of affairs—very limited affairs he was allowed, I might say—is in a tizzy about what to do, but has at least arranged the sale of the horses. And, to tie everything up in a bow, the *Melusine* is at anchor at Eastbourne awaiting another rental. That, I trust, covers all you had in mind."

Since Stephanie had not had any of that in mind,

she felt she had received a set-down, but a very satisfactory one in that it conveyed what she might have asked if she had put her mind to it. So she gave him a dazzling smile and said, "Thank you for being so—so comprehensive, my lord." With some regret she felt she could not ask a question for quite a while.

Lord Airde gave her a considering look and moved back to stand beside Sir Andrew. "We have come on a most serious occasion," he began slowly and suddenly looked a little awkward. "Stephanie, you had better go sit on that sofa so we can both address you."

"Do you wish me to leave the room?" Hester asked timidly as Stephanie rose, stalked to the green and white striped sofa, and with a rebellious glance plumped herself down in the exact center.

"Oh no, dear Miss Tinkham." Sir Andrew gave her a little bow. "You are our dear friend and have shared so much. We beg you to share this also." He went and took her hand and led her to a small *fauteuil* and gave her such a sweet smile that even at a distance Stephanie could see her blush.

Sir Andrew then placed himself carefully facing the empty portion of the sofa to the left and Airde faced the space on the right.

"This is ridiculous," Airde burst out with exasperation. "We are not on parade. We have consented to call on you together, Miss Langley, so neither of us will have an advantage over the other."

"We are friends," Sir Andrew interjected simply, "and I am deeply in his debt for many things as well as the care that has been given me in his home these past days."

"No one is in anyone's debt." Airde's voice roughened. "This just seemed a sensible arrangement. At lunch, by accident, we each revealed our intentions. But now it seems damned silly." He glowered at Stephanie as if it were all her fault.

Stephanie clasped her hands and gave a demure smile to the space between the two men. Whatever silly plan they shared she must humor them, or, better yet, put a halt to it now. "Then, since this is all so repulsive to you, why not simply postpone whatever it is you have to say until sometime when you are in a better humor? Or at least until Lord Airde is."

"I am in a perfectly good humor," Airde barked.

"Then stop glaring at me in such an infuriated fashion. It is not my fault you are here."

"Not a fault. Don't you understand . . ."

"No, no," Sir Andrew soothed. "We cannot postpone, Miss Langley. It is now we must speak, settle everything. I depart this evening."

Shocked and dismayed, Stephanie moved around to face him and found excitement, delight, anticipation lighting his face.

"Yes," he nodded. "Isn't it beyond belief? And it is thanks to Airde. My own regiment, too."

"Depart?" Stephanie interrupted. "What of your position at the Admiralty?"

"I should have known you would have some question," Airde cut her short. "The Admiralty people seem mystified by Maleby's disappearance, but accept his absence with equanimity and many are happy and hope it is permanent. That has nothing to do with Sir

Andrew, since he is in the army and his orders came from the War Department."

"I was informed I did not need to wait on Maleby's return. I confess I am astounded at my good fortune and that it came so quickly."

"What he is trying to tell you," Airde said a little acidly, "is that his posting has come and he leaves for Plymouth to rejoin his regiment. As you may gather, he is happy at the thought."

Sir Andrew put away his varied expressions. "Of course I am happy," he said soberly. "Any soldier would be."

"I understand that Sir Andrew is departing," Stephanie acknowledged, "and it is sad news for us. But why do you join him here at this particular time? It seems unnecessary."

"Of course it is necessary." Airde paused, then resumed. "I had no intention of disclosing what lay behind my presence, but I see it is necessary . . . I was coming home from Kent, and you were accompanying me constantly. That was yesterday. I had thought of you so steadily, and so deeply, that when I entered my house I was surprised you were not there to greet me. That told me I could wait no longer. If it had not been late I would have gone to you then. I looked at the empty hall and banged my fist on the table and said, and out loud, that I had given you enough time, and experience, and time with Seddon, for you to know which one you wished. I could not go on longer in my uncertainty. Then, today, we both mentioned we planned to call here, on you. Our intentions developed.

If I lose I am determined to apply for an immediate posting abroad."

"But . . ." Stephanie began, both flattered, providing she understood him correctly, and bewildered.

"We are using up our time," Sir Andrew pointed out gently. "Airde, you agreed to speak first because of rank and age."

"I am not sure I care for that last remark," Airde said a little caustically, "but I did so agree." He turned a quarter circle and raised one hand. "Control your instinct to ask more questions and make more comments, at least until we have both finished. And do show some feminine delicacy and appreciation of our positions."

He paused and suddenly he was grave. "We discovered, Sir Andrew and I, that we both had decided to speak to you this afternoon. Seddon is impelled by his departure and I by my own irresistible reasons. That presented an impasse, since neither of us was willing to take advantage of the other in any way. So we agreed on our present procedure, which I must say I find increasingly awkward."

"Well, I should think you would," Stephanie exploded angrily. "You neither of you have any sensitivity of feeling. Don't talk to me about mine. How can you subject a girl to such a humiliating situation?"

"Don't talk like a peahen . . ." Airde began.

"Not a humiliating situation." Seddon overrode him firmly. "Unusual, yes, but nothing humiliating in having two men who are in love with you offering you their hearts and hands."

At that note of reason Stephanie subsided, put her

hands on her cheeks and looked from one to the other. She could not believe what he had just announced.

"Thank you, Seddon," Airde began again, "for making clear the obvious which Miss Langley was about to overlook. I will try again. Stephanie," he took a step closer. As she looked up into his serious face, the eyes so intent and searching, she felt her heart give a strange leap. "I am here," he went on deliberately, "to beg you to do me the honor of becoming my wife." Watching her, he waited.

"Oh no," she gasped. This she had not expected in spite of all they had said. "I don't believe you."

"You must," he told her gently. "I do so beg you. Would you believe me more readily if I got down on one knee?"

"No, no." She shook her head. "That would indeed put your words beyond belief."

"Then I won't," he agreed, still serious, and turned to Seddon. "You must speak before she can make any serious answer."

"And most happy to." Seddon's pleasant voice, a little strained and uncertain, caught her before she could give thought to this astonishing scene. "Miss Langley, I have loved you since the first time I saw you at Mrs Riffton's. You would make me the happiest man on earth if you would do me the honor of allowing me to marry you."

Mesmerized by words she had never expected to hear, Stephanie gazed at the beautiful anxious face, and a sincerity that was not to be doubted.

"Well done," Airde approved. "I forgot that bit about loving from the first moment. A nice touch." He shook his head. "I couldn't have said that, though, even if I had thought of it. It wouldn't have been true."

"Of course it wouldn't," Stephanie agreed indignantly. "You never saw me at our first encounter."

"But I heard you. I remembered your charming voice and also what you said."

"Her voice *is* charming," Sir Andrew broke in, "but I fell in love with every aspect of Miss Langley at the first moment."

Wide-eyed, Stephanie stared at him. "Oooooh," she breathed.

"But my love grew each time I met her," Airde pointed out. "It grew and burgeoned steadily, and very quickly, I might add. You wouldn't want to be a girl who is a *coup de foudre*, Stephanie."

She transferred her gaze. "Oh, I would. What a delightful thought. Any girl would."

"Not like you to run with the crowd that way, my dear." He shook his head but for a flash his eyes were amused. "All right, Seddon, that trick is yours."

"Only the truth," Seddon said with dignity.

Stephanie looked from one to the other and found herself clutching her hair. "You are both quite mad," she gasped, "though it is not apparent except for your demented words."

"You do not do yourself justice," Airde said to her with maddening kindness. "You are quite attractive enough to overpoweringly engage the affections of any man, and of an intelligence and character that would enslave any man wise enough to appreciate them."

Stephanie's mouth fell open. "You are jesting," she managed to sputter. "I do not care for it."

"He is not," Seddon contradicted her emphatically, "We are both agreed on your mind and character and complete desirability as a wife. Furthermore," and his voice strengthened, "though I have not mentioned this before, I not only love you but need you. I have learned with both pain and pleasure that I am not adequately acquainted with the world, the social and general world, not the military, to manage my life with any degree of satisfaction for myself and my wife. You are so clever, wise, you could assist, guide, manage . . . And I need you to think of during my next two years while I am in the army. You will no doubt reside at your grandfather's home. I can dream of you there, enjoying country life, and waiting for my return. You will inspire me. And when the two years are over, and I come back to you, how happy we will be. If you love me, that is. You do love me, don't you?" His anxiety deepened.

"She doesn't," Airde contradicted roughly. "It is true she has always said you were beautiful and that she wished you were her Sir Andrew. And that, my girl, put me off and misguided me for a while, particularly after I found he is a good man. That, and all the others you had dangling in an infuriating fashion. But I would not give up. She loves *me,* and she knows it. She has—responded. There is a tie between us that will endure beyond a moonlight moment."

As Stephanie recalled that moment she felt herself blushing. She looked at him appealingly and found him watching with a tenderness such as she had never imagined. "You agree," he almost whispered, and, remembering again, she nodded.

"I do not know to what you refer," Seddon said carefully. "But I must point out we do not have a clear-cut answer."

Stephanie folded her hands and looked from one to the other. "You cannot mean me to make up my mind now between you," she began with what she felt was the utmost good sense. "Since I must believe this is not a farce you have concocted, you must have some other intention. No girl could settle the most important matter of her life at such speed and in such a way."

"You must." Airde's voice was stern. "We have explained the reasons for our precipitate action, which should be extremely flattering to you. You have seen a sufficiency of us both over these past weeks, and in very varied circumstances, to know us, our characters, our attitudes, far better than is the lot of most girls today to know their suitors. Your heart knows. Consult it. We must leave within a half hour, for I am driving Seddon to the coach for Plymouth. We must both know your decision before we depart . . ."

Stephanie leaned back against the sofa and again looked from one to the other. They were so handsome, each in his own way. To use Airde's phrase, she knew they were both good men. Both had been such good friends, she had enjoyed their company, their adventures. But . . . For a moment her sense of outrage rose and she longed to tell them this was no way to woo anyone and to go away. But then they would, being proud men, and she would never see them again and that she could not bear. For another moment, she wished she could consult with someone, her mother, her grandfather, Cousin Doria, but realized each would say she must decide for herself. She looked again. Their expressions were serious, watching her, waiting for her words. There was a pleading look in Seddon's blue eyes and the words "I need you" hung between them, blotting out the moonlight. And she knew he would need her.

She sat up straight and dropped her eyes. "I assure you I am very conscious of the extreme honor both you gentlemen are doing me in spite of the—the irregularity of the manner. Lord Airde, I—I cannot deny anything you have said." His face began to relax its tension and he brightened. "But," she went on, a little forlornly, "you do not need me as Sir Andrew does. You have everything, a person and manner that can charm the world when you wish, position, money, esteem, a career, everything you need. You have no need of Stephanie Langley." His eyes turned impenetrable.

She looked to her right. "Sir Andrew, I have long been sensible of the pleasure of your company and your worth and your dignity in a world strange to you. I know I could be of—of help to you when you return, and that our life together, when you leave the army to live on your estate, would be most agreeable. So—so I accept your most kind offer."

"Stephanie!" He glowed with happiness. "You make me the happiest of men!" He took a step forward and halted.

Apprehensively, Stephanie turned to look at Airde. He was very composed and bowed with dignity. "One cannot dispute a lady, ma'am, and your word to me is law. Seddon, congratulations. I will await you in the lower room." He turned briskly and started for the door.

Involuntarily Stephanie's hand went out toward him. "Ohhh," she breathed at the straight receding back, at the swiftness with which he had accepted her decision ... What had she done? And beyond repair. For she had given her word. In silence he reached the door and halted, turned and looked back at her.

Then he was striding across the room. "No, by gad. I can dispute anyone. I cannot allow you to be bird-brained about this, my girl. You are quite right. We should have allowed you more time and it is no one's fault we cannot. You have had no chance to think, to allow your heart and your head to overthrow those sensibilities.

"Seddon is an admirable and endearing man, I grant. But have you ever laughed with him as you have with me? Have you thought what his needing you entails? Two years, my girl, of roosting in Dorset, managing the house, a little gardening, teaching Sunday school, waiting for a letter that may come once a month. Just waiting, in reality, while life and the world go by. And when the waiting is over, for I have no doubt he will return safely, you transfer the country life to the woods and fields of Suffolk and wait on the weather to provide you with conversation, along with the state of the farms. No, you enjoy life, people, the world around you too much to bury yourself forever."

The word "forever" rang like a knell. She watched him, a light growing in her eyes. How right he was about country life. She did love it, but not, not for the rest of her life. There was so much else to see and do.

Airde was nearly in a rage. "I won't allow it, do you understand? I have had my heart and mind fixed on you ever since our second encounter, when I found you searching through my desk with such enjoyment at the adventure. You gave me pause with your avowed *tendre* for Seddon. I saw you again and vowed to have you. Then I felt I should give you time, all the time you needed to make up your mind. I lost some confidence, but told myself you would be safe with him, but I hoped. Just now you knocked me to pieces when you accepted him."

"You did not show it," she gasped.

"Of course not." He paced away angrily and came back and glowered at her. "Stephanie, you would be so *bored* with him. Think of all the things we have enjoyed together—and there is so much more . . . Forget all that balderdash about his needing you. Granted he does. He needs any sensible wife to manage him. What he will need even more is an heiress, for his estate cannot support even a modest gentleman in fashion. He'll find an heiress two years from now, no need to concern yourself on that.

"And as for my not needing you. Gammon, my dear nitwit. I need you far more than he does or ever will. You said I have everything. But you left out the most important thing in my life. I don't have you. Without you my life, for all those silly things you so carefully listed, would be dead dull, if you are not beside me to enjoy it, for me to love and cherish and laugh with and make life whole. I love you to desperation. Don't you understand that? Then stop allowing those female sensibilities, which are only an excuse to do what you think is noble and self-sacrificing, to have any sway. Now come here." He was in front of her, holding out his hands.

She put hers in his and came up so swiftly and so gladly he laughed. "I knew you had good sense. All you need is a little firmness. And I know you love me."

As he brought her toward him she heard Hester saying very clearly, "If you should wish to find a friend when you return in two years, Sir Andrew, I will be waiting."

Airde paused and they both looked to the fireplace. Sir Andrew had walked there and, hands behind his back, stood gazing down at the empty hearth. Hester rose and approached him, paused, then softly touched his arm. "I would be happy to correspond with you if you should care to hear occasionally from a friend while you are away," she told the bowed head carefully.

"How kind of you," he said slowly. "Yes, I would be pleased to have letters from a friend."

"Then come with me to the library and tell me how I must address you," she suggested, more strongly.

There was a moment of silence, then he turned and she laid her hand on his arm and began to walk to the door. He went with her as if oblivious of the two remaining.

"How very tactful of her," Airde murmured. "She will make just the wife he needs." He looked down at Stephanie. "But we aren't waiting," he exulted, "are we, dear heart?" and began to kiss her gently, then more firmly. "Tell me you love me," he managed a little unevenly in a few moments. "You must say it."

"I do love you, most desperately too." She was not surprised to find her voice was shaking. "I have for so long." How satisfying to be able to say it out loud to him.

"A month is too long to wait, my darling," and kissed her again.

"Yes," Stephanie gasped when she could. "Yes. No. But oh Airde, what will your family say, for I have neither position or dowry."

"No girl ever needed them less. Family? Why," he threw back his head and laughed, "I wager Great-Aunt Di gave that outrageous party and insulted me at the end just to bring me up short. She was always devious and skillful. And you must begin saying Esham, my love, instantly."

"Yes, Esham, but why?"

"She liked you, and I have a feeling she had a *tendre* for your grandfather. She wished to do something for you—and for me."

"So we would both have to make up our minds?"

"And it's too late for us to change. And I'll tell you another thing, my girl, you've had your last adventure."

"No." She put her hands against his chest and shoved a very little to look up into his face.

"What do you mean no?" he asked with what she realized was a dangerous quiet. "Your adventures are over."

"No . . ." she began again.

He pulled her closer, "I'll teach you not to say no to me." There was a flash in his eyes that stopped her heart and he was kissing her differently, fiercely and demanding, and her heart leaped and she answered. "There," he muttered against her lips.

She moved her head back. "I said no," she told him breathlessly, "because my adventures aren't over. Being married to you is going to be the most wonderful adventure I could have." And she welcomed his kiss.

Sylvia Thorpe

Romantic tales of adventure, intrigue and gallantry.